Where the Heart Belongs

A collection of short stories

by

Sridevi Pudipeddi

I want to thank all the people in the front line providing essential services during the Coronavirus pandemic of 2019-2020.

To my friend Diann Marten for always being there for me.

We encourage you to support research in infectious diseases. Here are a few organizations that are helping research and support:

https://www.mayo.edu/research/departments-divisions/department-internal-medicine/division-infectious-diseases/overview

https://www.hopkinsmedicine.org/infectious-diseases/research/

https://www.tuftsmedicalcenter.org/patient-care-services/departments-and-services/infectious-disease/research-clinical-trials/india-research

https://www.globalgiving.org/projects/coronavirus-relief-fund/

https://www.who.int/emergencies/diseases/novel-coronavirus-2019/donate

https://www.pmindia.gov.in/en/about-pm-cares-fund/

Acknowledgements:

Thank you Ravi Chityala for creating the book cover.

References of the links that were used to create the book cover:

https://www.pngfuel.com/free-png/bjjnz

pxhere.com/en/photo/1603819

Table of Contents

Country Above Love

Saleem and Geeta didn't mean to fall in love. But love happens when you least expect it. It creeps up suddenly. Love doesn't look at logic, or at backgrounds and least of all, religion.

Geeta was from a very conservative South Indian family that went to a temple every Saturday. Saleem bought goats for his family every Eid. That said it all. Their paths would never have crossed if it hadn't been for that day when he walked into the coffee shop. Geeta wondered if destiny chose our loved ones for us. Did we have any role to play at all?

She looked at her watch. Saleem was late. They met every Thursday at five pm. Sometimes at the cafe, sometimes in his car, sometimes in places that she could never tell her friends about. They would never understand. Their conversations lasted for hours. Saleem made her happy.

Suddenly her phone beeped with a message from Saleem, "On my way. Have something important to tell you."

Geeta stared at it and realized she had knots in her stomach. Thoughts flooded her mind. What did he want to tell her?

Waiting in the coffee shop, her mind drifted to the first time when they met five years ago. *She was in the final year of her master's and was returning from college in a bus when four unruly teenagers got in. They not only refused to pay their bus fare but started calling the female bus conductor by nasty names. "If you can't pay, then you can't ride on this bus," the conductor said.*

"This is not your father's bus," one of them shouted back. He got up and tried to slap her. The conductor ducked.

A young man rushed to the boy and held him back. "Someone, call the police," he shouted. Geeta recognized him from the coffee shop that she frequented with her friends.

The bus driver stopped the bus and called the emergency police number.

The boy's friends made their way out and ran away.

"Good that you held him," the driver said to the young man.

"How can we let him treat her so poorly?" the young man asked. "She was just doing her job."

The boy held his head low.

After ten minutes, Geeta could hear the police siren.

The police came and took statements from the eye witnesses and took the boy with them.

Geeta joined the other passengers in the bus to applaud the bold chap.

When she got down at her stop, she noticed that the same young man also got down at her stop. He smiled at her. "What you did in the bus was nice," she said nodding her head. His chivalry made an impression on her.

"We have to stand up and stop such behavior. Otherwise they will never stop," he said.

"Do you live in this neighborhood?"

"Yes, near the mosque," he replied. "Where do you live?"

"Near the bank."

"Your name?" he asked leaning forward.

"I am Geeta."

"That's a very nice name," he said, extending his hand. "I am Saleem." They shook hands.

"Are you studying?" she asked.

"Yes, I am training to be a chartered accountant," he said. "I am taking the final exams next month. And you?"

"I will be earning a Master's in Bioinformatics soon," she said.

"Bioinformatics, I heard it is an up and coming field."

She smiled. "My cousin is a chartered accountant."

"Nice."

They walked up to her street. "Maybe we will run into each other again," he said. "Bye."

"Yes, bye." She took a few steps and hoped he would ask her for her phone number.

"Geeta," he said.

Her name from his mouth sounded sweet.

"Yes," she said, turning eagerly.

"Do you want to exchange phone numbers?" he said.

"Yes, sure," she said and pulled out her phone. As they exchanged their phone numbers, her lips gave away a smile. "If you are interested, I can introduce you to my cousin who is already a practicing chartered accountant."

"Yes, that would be great."

The following week, Geeta introduced Saleem to her cousin.

"Your friend Saleem is a smart guy," her cousin said to her when she was visiting him.

"Really?"

"He is getting trained at one of the top accounting firms," her cousin said with wide eyes.

Geeta was happy to hear that her new acquaintance had formed an agreeable impression on her cousin.

In the following weeks, she and Saleem took the same bus home.

After his exams, they started to hang out. "So you don't mind going out with a Muslim?" he asked her.

"No," she shook her head shyly. "And you don't mind going out with a Hindu?"

"I don't mind," he said.

"How can we brand and box people because they are from a particular religion?" she asked.

"Honestly, I never understand all the fuss about religion," he said.

She then knew she found the right man.

The noise from the coffee grinder broke her chain of thought. She turned around and smiled at her surroundings. The aroma of freshly ground coffee engulfed her. There was something about the coffee shop that made it their favorite place.

Today they planned to meet for dinner but Saleem asked to meet for coffee instead.

She overheard someone in the coffee shop ask, "How can you?" and then she remembered one particular conversation that she had with her mother last year.

"How can you embrace his eating habits?" her mother asked sobbing inconsolably. After being together for four years, she and Saleem decided to get married. He had joined an accounting firm and she was working at a research lab. It was the perfect time to start a new life. But as expected her parents were not thrilled about him being a Muslim.

"I am not going to become a meat eater," Geeta said. "Please Amma stop crying and listen to me."

"How can I stop crying?" her mother demanded. "Don't you see? I will be losing my daughter. You will change your name."

"I am not changing my name," Geeta said loudly.

"You are not?" Her mother asked.

"That's what I am trying to say." Geeta put her hand on her mother's shoulder. "I will continue to be a Hindu and he will continue to be a Muslim. We are not going to change anything for the marriage. We accept each other as we are."

"Is that true?" her mother squinted.

"Since some married people were converting into Islam to have multiple wives, recently Supreme Court ruled that changing religion for marriage is illegal."

"So, you will still be Geeta." Her mother kissed her on her cheek.

"Yes Amma, your Geeta."

They both hugged.

After gaining her mother's approval, Geeta went to convince her father.

"If you marry into a Muslim family, who will marry your sister?" her father asked.

"Appa, I have to fulfill my destiny and my sister has to fulfill hers," Geeta said, not losing her cool. "You should welcome my decision on its own without strings attached."

"In which faith will you raise your children?" her father asked.

"They will be exposed to both faiths," Geeta said. Many such discussions followed. But when her parents met Saleem their opposition disappeared. He made a point to spend time with them. Her parents' first-hand interactions with Saleem dispelled their worries. Even her sister bonded with her to be brother-in-law.

Saleem didn't have to convince his parents as much. Some of his relatives were married into other religions and cultures. So that made it easy.

They decided to have a civil service marriage, followed by a reception. However, her mother and Saleem's mother made plans for evening ceremonies too.

Saleem tapped on her hand and said, "Hello."

"Hi."

"Are you daydreaming?" he asked.

"Yeah."

"Sorry I am a little late. What do you want to get?"

They returned to the table with beverages and sat at the end of the coffee shop.

"Why did you want to meet for coffee instead of dinner?" she asked looking into his eyes.

"I will tell you soon, how was your day?"

"They made me in charge of recruiting interns," she said.

"Congratulations."

"Thanks. How was yours?"

"It was okay."

"Saleem, are you hiding something from me?"

"Geeta, I will never hide anything from you."

"Then why are you so sad? Are you having second thoughts about our wedding?" In the last five years, she never doubted their commitment and it was stupid to doubt it now. Their wedding was scheduled for next week and she didn't want any surprises.

"I don't have any second thoughts," he said and held her hands. "You are the best thing that ever happened to me."

"I am sorry for doubting your commitment," she apologized. "Then what is it?"

He sighed. "My sister ran away from home."

"What?"

"Yes, she and my cousin, Ameera decided to run away."

"When did this happen?"

"They both went to see my grandparents in Delhi and were supposed to reach Delhi yesterday afternoon. However, they never arrived. In the evening, my grandmother called to inquire about the girls."

"Why didn't you tell me?"

"I didn't want you to worry." He gently squeezed her hand.

"Have you reported it to the police?"

He shook his head. "I know where they went," he said.

"Where did they go?"

"They went to join ISIS." He burst into tears.

"What?" She had heard about ISIS but, she never thought that someone she knew would be so brainwashed that they would join an Islamic militia which was known as one of the most dangerous groups in the world. "I am so sorry to hear that." The news about ISIS barbaric acts flashed in her memory. This was the first time someone she knew took such a drastic step of joining the most notorious organization. The far reach of the militia scared her.

"It is hard to believe that those two girls decided to go fight for something so radical and so wrong," he said looking down.

"But why didn't you inform the police? Don't you think they might be able to help?"

"I will." He composed himself and took a deep breath. "My sister left a letter on her desk. All this time, I never paid attention to what the girls did. Yesterday, I hacked into my sister's computer and found out that they both watched an ungodly number of radical videos. They created fake twitter accounts and openly expressed their support of ISIS."

"Aren't they too young to join such a group?"

"Unfortunately, the group has been influencing young people all around the world," he said.

"How are your parents?"

"They are devastated. My mother hasn't stopped crying. My father blames himself for not accompanying my sister to go see my grandparents."

"I want to see your parents."

***

They found his parents in the dining area. His father sat slumped in a chair and his mother's eyes were swollen and red. It didn't look like they had eaten anything the whole day.

"Let me make you something to eat," Geeta said and opened the refrigerator. She picked out a few vegetables and started preparing some food.

"Any news?" his father asked hopefully.

Saleem shook his head.

"Ameera's parents will be coming shortly," his mother informed him.

"What had gotten into these girls?" his mother asked. "Mariam was too lazy even to clean her room and now she wants to fight. I can't believe kids these days. By her age I was married."

"This is my fault," Saleem's father said. "I trusted her and she chose to make a fool out of me."

"Papa, it's nobody's fault," Saleem said.

"It is of course my fault," his father insisted. "My child decides to join the most extreme organization in the world and how can I not be responsible?"

"Saleem is right," his mother said, dabbing her eyes with her chunni. "We are good people. We have taught good things to our children. See how Saleem has turned out."

"Dear Mariam why did you do this?" his father asked, looking at her picture that was on the dining table.

"Papa, I think we should inform the police," Saleem suggested.

"I know. I asked your inspector uncle to accompany us. He will be here any minute."

"Uncle, please eat something before you go," Geeta suggested.

His father nodded.

***

Geeta stayed with Saleem's mother while the men went to the police station.

"I am sorry that all this is happening right before your wedding," his mother apologized.

"It is not that it is happening before my wedding, the fact that it happened at all is what is making me sad," Geeta said. "I would have never guessed that Mariam would do such a thing. All my interactions with Mariam were friendly and funny. Mariam seemed like someone who wanted to strike out on her own in a good way."

***

The men returned with sullen faces.

"Sister, I am so sorry," the inspector uncle said to Saleem's mother and took a seat. "My colleague has photographs of Mariam and Ameera. We will definitely find them." His phone rang. He took the call. He listened intently and then ended the conversation. "It looks like our girls and ten others have left for Egypt," he informed everybody in the room.

"Egypt!" Saleem's mother started crying again. "My Mariam can't do this." She pressed her hand on the table and rose. She went to her husband and held his hands in hers. "Please go get our child," she begged.

Saleem's father stared at her. "Yes, yes, I will go get her," he said, gaining strength. "Yes, I will bring our daughter back." He turned to the inspector and asked, "Can we find out more about their itinerary?"

"I will inform the Indian intelligence office and I hope they can contact their Egyptian counterparts," the inspector said and rose.

"Papa, give me a second," Saleem said and turned to Geeta.

Geeta's heart skittered.

"Geeta, can we talk?" Saleem asked.

She nodded. They went to the balcony.

"Can I go with my father to find Mariam?" Saleem requested.

Tears flooded her eyes. "ISIS is run by savages," the tears came down her cheeks. "It was in the news that, when a recruit's mother went in person and begged her son to leave the group. The recruit not only refused …," she closed her eyes and couldn't complete the sentence.

"To leave the group but he beheaded her instead," Saleem completed her sentence. "I read it too. I applaud that mother for risking everything to save her son. It is a pity that he didn't deserve her love." He stared into the blackness enveloping their backyard. "Intercepting Mariam before she joins the group is our only hope. However, everything will change if she joins the group before we can reach her."

She looked into his eyes. "I am so scared," she said. Within hours, her life had turned upside down. Then she remembered something, "I know someone who lives in Egypt," she said.

"Who?" Saleem asked.

Geeta immediately called her father's cell. When her father answered, she explained what had happened. She worried how her parents would react to this disturbing news. "I will come to Saleem's place and talk to him and his parents," her father said. She sighed with relief.

***

After talking to Saleem and his parents, Geeta's father said, "One of my cousins lives in Egypt. He owns a company there. Saleem, I will introduce you to him. I hope he can help you."

"Thank you Uncle," Saleem said.

"That is very kind of you," Saleem's father said to Geeta's father.

"Please don't thank me," Geeta's father said. "We are family now, we need to do everything to find Mariam as soon as we can."

Her father's kind words warmed Geeta's heart, tears swelled in her eyes.

***

"I am scared too," Saleem said. "But I need to do this for my family, for my country."

"I understand," Geeta said. "I would do anything to stop my sister from ruining her life."

"Tomorrow, I am going to apply for an expedited Egyptian visa," Saleem said. "Your father's cousin invited me to stay with him and his family."

"That is kind of him," Geeta observed. "How will you find Mariam?"

"I don't know," Saleem replied. "But with your support, I am sure I can figure something out."

"Promise me that you will be careful," she said.

"If something happens to me," his voice choked.

"Don't say such things," she said. "I am sure you will return safely."

Where the Heart Belongs

The architecture of the Hawa Mahal in Jaipur India had captured Meera with its beauty. She found the palace with the numerous small windows delightful. As she clicked her camera to take another picture, her husband, Dev said, "Don't you get tired of taking pictures?"

She moved the camera away from her face for a brief moment and then smiled at his naïve question.

"Will you be done soon?" Dev asked.

"Sure." From a window, she took a picture of the street.

By one o' clock they were outside on the side road next to the main street. They tried to locate their taxi when they heard a baby crying inconsolably. Except for a row of waiting taxis and a few tourists they saw no signs of any babies around.

"Who is crying?" She turned her head to see.

"I don't see any babies in the vicinity." Dev said.

As soon as he saw them, their taxi driver, Shyam, got out and opened the back door.

"Do you hear a baby crying?" Meera asked him.

"Yes madam."

"I don't see anyone around with a child." Dev said.

Noticing that his customers were reluctant to get in, "Do you want me to find out?" he asked.

"Yes," Meera said.

Shyam closed the door and went up the road. He walked past a trash dump and could immediately sense that the sound came from the dump. He hesitantly turned towards his customers who were anxiously waiting for him. He waved and signaled them to come over.

As Dev got nearer the repugnant smell made him cover his nose.

Meera took a step closer and said, "I don't see anyone."

"I think the baby is in there," Shyam said pointing his finger to a big cylindrical trash container.

Meera and Dev looked at each other in confusion and in unison said, "What?"

"I think someone dumped their baby," Shyam said in a compassionate tone.

"We have to rescue the baby now," Meera said urgently.

"Yes." Dev quickly handed his backpack to his wife and he peeked into the can, but the noise was coming from outside. He went around and saw a tiny leg hanging out of a cane basket. "Oh God," he said as he picked up the basket and ran back to the other side of the street. He took the baby out and sat down. He rocked the child hoping it would stop crying.

Meera knelt down. She stroked the child's head. "I can't believe someone left their baby here." She scanned the area around the trash can. "The heartless person didn't even cover the poor child; they left the baby with only a diaper!"

"I think we should call the police," Shyam took out his cell phone and dialed the police emergency number 1-0-0.

***

In less than ten minutes, the Jaipur police along with an ambulance came to the scene.

"Did you call us?" asked the police officer as he came near the trio, a couple of constables were behind him.

Shyam took the lead and explained what had happened.

The police placed a few orange cones around the area. The constables wore gloves and started searching the container.

Dev handed the baby to the paramedics.

"We couldn't find anything," said one of the constables.

The paramedics briefed the police officer and left immediately.

"Sir, is it a girl child?" Shyam asked the officer.

"Yes," the officer nodded. "It looks like the baby is only a few days old."

"Are you taking her to the main government hospital?" Shyam asked.

"Yes."

"Do you think we can go see her in a day or two?" Meera asked the police officer.

"Sure, I will tell the hospital about you."

"Thank you," Meera said.

The police officer and constables left.

"After witnessing the gruesome reality of an unwanted child, I am in no mood for more sightseeing today," Dev said, "Do you want to grab something to eat and go to our hotel?"

"Yes. I feel sad too," replied Meera.

***

Later in the evening, Meera sat next to the window in their hotel room watching the street traffic and the passersby.

"Whenever you are up to it, we can start packing our luggage," Dev said.

Meera nodded.

"See how those parents are holding their daughter's hand while they are walking." Her eyes followed them until they went around the corner and she couldn't see them anymore.

He took a seat opposite to her and took her hand. "Why do you look sad? Is everything okay?"

"I am finding it hard that someone had a baby and then they decided to throw her away."

"Maybe they didn't have resources to raise the child," Dev said.

"Or maybe they left the child because it is a girl."

Dev looked away.

As shameful as it was to admit, lately it has become a common practice in some parts of India to abandon newborn girls. In a country where women goddesses are revered, having a girl child is sometimes considered a financial burden or a curse. He took her hands into his and squeezed them lightly.

"Do you want to go buy souvenirs? Maybe that will take your mind off the baby." He asked.

"Okay. That's a good idea."

"Then let's go." He tried to pull her from the chair.

"I can get up. But first we have to make a list."

Dev reached for the notepad and pen that were on the nightstand.

***

"This place is so crowded," Meera said looking at the sea of people in a narrow street.

"I guess everyone is looking for special deals," Dev said. "We can check out the shops in the front."

She reluctantly followed him.

As soon as she touched a scarf that hung on the side of a shop, the shop owner said, "Madam, you made a good choice. This scarf is handmade and hand dyed."

"Please wait, we are still looking," Dev said.

"Sure sir, please take your time. I sell the best products for a reasonable price."

Meera felt a tap on her arm and she turned and saw a girl no more than ten in ragged clothes and unkempt hair next to her. "Madam, please give me some money," the girl asked with an open palm while the other arm dangled from the oversized salwar that she wore.

Meera could tell that the girl hadn't showered in a few days and maybe didn't have a home to go to.

"Hey girl, don't bother my customers," the shop owner shouted. "Why are you always hovering around my shop? If you don't run off now, I will report you to the police."

The girl still held the palm in a hope of some loose change.

Meera dug into her purse but before she could fetch the change, the owner opened the side door and went towards the girl.

The girl ran into the maze of people.

"The city is infested with beggars and the police are doing nothing," the owner muttered as he came back inside.

"You didn't have to be so rude. The poor girl asked me, not you." Meera frowned. "Dev, let's go to a different shop."

"Madam, I do feel sorry for them but what can I do? I am an owner of a small shop and I have to provide for my own family," he said in an apologetic tone. He lifted the top of a wooden box and took out a photograph of his family and held it towards Meera. "See madam, I have two daughters. They both go to school. Please madam, don't leave my shop. I just didn't want anybody to bother my customers."

The picture of the two girls calmed Meera. But she wondered about the future of the girl child that they helped rescue today. *What will happen to her? Where will she live? Who is going to care for her?* These questions bothered Meera but she had to finish shopping. They planned to do their shopping in Jaipur; so that in Kochi they would have plenty of time to meet family and friends before they headed back to the US in two weeks.

Overwhelmed with the events, Meera was tired of arguing. She counted the number of women on their gift list and picked dyed scarves for all of them. Dev picked carved wooden elephants for the men.

As they were carrying their bags to their hotel, Meera was grateful that she bought lightweight scarves instead of bangles that were the region's popular souvenir.

"Can I ask you something?" She asked.

"Sure."

"I know we can have our own kids. But can we adopt the baby that we found today?" Meera asked.

"Absolutely," Dev responded.

Not expecting such a quick positive response, Meera said, "Are you sure?"

"Yes, I am sure."

"I mean, don't you want to think about it?" She asked.

"What is there to think? We love children and I am sure we will love this baby as our own."

In the middle of the street, they dropped their bags and hugged each other.

***

Next day morning, Shyam met the couple at the hotel lobby to take them to the airport. Not seeing their luggage he asked, "Sir, where are your suitcases?"

"We decided to stay for a few more days."

"That's wonderful sir. Where do you want to go today?" Shyam asked.

"We first want to go to the hospital where the baby was taken," Dev said, turning towards Meera.

She grinned.

"Sure Sir," Shyam said.

***

At the hospital, the head nurse took them to the neonatal intensive care unit on the second floor of the hospital. After crossing rows and rows of infants, she stopped at a bed and said, "This is the baby."

"Why is she here?" Meera asked. "Is she ill?"

"She has malaria. The poor child has a lot of mosquito bites on her body. She is also under-weight. So, we are monitoring her."

Oblivious to her surroundings, the baby smiled at her rescuers.

The baby's infectious smile captivated Meera. She felt an instant bond.

"Nurse, we want to talk to someone in the child protection services," Dev said.

"Sure, I can take you to their office. Every government run hospital has a child protection officer in house so they can get involved right away."

Offices on the fifth floor looked under-furnished and old. The head nurse took them to a desk and introduced them to the child protection services officer, Ms. Keys.

Meera and Dev took seats facing the officer while Shyam sat on a small stool that was borrowed from another desk.

"It is nice to see that you went out of your way to rescue the baby," Ms. Keys said.

"That is the least we could do," Dev said.

"I wish we had more Good Samaritans like you and your wife," the officer said and smiled at him and Meera. "What can I do for you?"

"We want to adopt the baby," Meera said eagerly.

"Are you sure?" Ms. Keys asked.

"Yes," Dev and Meera said in unison.

"Do you have children of your own?" Ms. Keys asked.

"No, we don't," Dev replied.

"I mean raising a child is very demanding. Did you really think through this?"

Meera expected that the officer would hug them and hand them the baby right away. She couldn't comprehend the officer's concerns. "Why are you asking us these questions?"

"We ask these questions to every family that is planning to adopt children," Ms. Keys said. "I am sorry if I sound rude but these are very important questions. Some people might have the right intentions but adopting a child is a big undertaking. I want to know that you are aware of parental responsibilities."

Meera's eyebrow knot eased. She nodded.

Ms. Keys opened her desk drawer and took out an adoption questionnaire. She filled in the couple's name and asked, "Where do you live?"

"In the US," Dev said.

"Are you planning to take the baby with you?"

"Yes," Meera said.

Ms. Keys scribbled in her notebook. "Mrs. Nayar, I don't want to scare you but I heard that childcare is expensive in the US. Is that true?"

Dev and Meera looked at each other and smiled.

"Yes," Meera said. "But since we both work full-time; I am sure we will be able to afford it."

"That's good. I need the documents that are on this list. After you submit them, I can process your application." Ms. Keys gave them the list along with a brand-new application form.

Meera and Dev stared at the list in disbelief. It would take them several days to get all the required documents.

"Ms. Keys, is there any way we could expedite the process?" Dev asked. "I mean, can you tell us the most important documents on the list?"

"The reason we are making this unusual request is because we will be leaving for the US in a couple of weeks and we want to take the baby with us," Meera explained.

"I will see what I can do."

Meera and Dev sighed and profusely thanked the officer.

"Don't thank me yet," Ms. Keys said. "I would still need copies of your passport, financials and a one-page essay on why you want to adopt."

"We will get the documents soon," Dev said as he got up.

"I will see you then."

***

It had been three days since they submitted the application and they were anxiously waiting for Ms. Keys' reply. Meera checked her phone to make sure it was working.

"Meera, don't be so anxious," Dev said.

"Waiting is boring." Meera grunted.

"Me too," Dev said typing away on his keyboard. They had already seen the major attractions in Jaipur and were ready to leave. Meanwhile Dev started working remotely.

"I envy you. Your work is keeping you busy while I am worrying."

"Why don't you go out?"

"What if I am out and I miss Ms. Keys' call?"

"If she can't reach you then I am sure she will call me."

Right then her phone rang. She pressed the accept button and said hello. As she spoke she smiled at Dev. He rose from his seat and came close to her. "We will be right there," she said and hung-up. "Congratulations! We are parents," she said and hugged him.

***

The twenty-minute ride to the hospital felt like eternity. Since Shyam was instrumental in finding the baby, Meera and Dev decided to take him along.

"Mr. and Mrs. Nayar, I am so happy for you," Ms. Keys said and handed the adoption papers to the couple.

"Thank you for expediting the process," Meera said.

"Sometimes things just work out and I am glad I was of some help. Let's go to the lower level where the baby awaits you."

As they came to the lower level, the couple was happy to see the baby in a private room. When the nurse tried to change the baby's clothes, the sleeping child woke up and started crying.

"We bought a new dress for her," Meera said and pulled out a purple frock with white flowers from her duffle bag. She looked at the crying baby and held her for the first time. In her hands, the baby felt like her own. She wiped the baby's tears with a cloth and soon the baby stopped crying and as destiny would have it the baby innocently smiled at her new mother. This was the first time the baby was welcomed into this world. Meera turned to Dev and nudged him to join.

"Yes," Dev said and for the first time on the trip, he clicked the camera to capture the treasure. He then handed the camera to Shyam and joined his family. "Jaya, I am your dad," he introduced himself to his daughter.

"Jaya is really a nice name sir," Shyam said. "Is it because she is from Jaipur?"

"No, because she is a survivor," Dev said.

Her mother's earrings captivated Jaya. Meera patiently unbuttoned her daughter's single piece dress and like an experienced mother slipped on the new frock.

"She is very light," Dev said as he lifted Jaya. "Nurse, is this normal?"

"She is a little underweight, I am sure she will gain weight soon," the nurse assured. "The good news is her fever subsided and she is responding well to the anti-malaria medication."

They thanked Ms. Keys and with their treasure in tow they took leave.

***

The queue outside the US consulate was long and winding. Even though Meera, Dev and Jaya came on time for the visa appointment, it seemed like they would be late. After passing through the security check, all their items were searched again.

After waiting for an hour in the long waiting area, their turn came. They stood at a glass window and on the other side was an officer.

The officer greeted them and said, "Please give me the adoption document and your visa papers."

Dev ruffled through the file and took the relevant papers and slid them through the small opening.

The officer took the papers and said, "Congratulations on becoming parents."

"Thank you," Dev said.

The officer studied the papers carefully. "It looks like you both have applied for your green card and are working on H1. Is this correct?"

"Yes sir." Dev said.

The officer turned to his computer and with a few mouse clicks was looking at Dev and Meera's past visa appointments. He sighed, shook his head and said, "I am afraid, we can't issue a visa for your daughter."

"Why?" Dev and Meera asked simultaneously.

"According to the US immigration law, since your green card process is underway, you can't legally bring your adopted child to the US." "Really?" Meera's heart sank. How can we return to the US without our child? What are we going to do?

"I am sorry but I can't do anything," the officer said. "On the bright side, you can take your daughter to the US once you get your green cards."

Dev and Meera looked at each other in disbelief. The officer's point caught them off guard. They thought getting a visa for Jaya was a formality but didn't expect it to become a hassle.

***

"Don't worry Meera, we can take care of Jaya," Nalini, Meera's mother said, stroking Jaya's hair as she slept on her lap. They were in Meera's parents' backyard enjoying a quiet sunset.

"Mom, I can't expect you to care for my child in your retirement," Meera said.

"I understand your reservations but someone has to look after Jaya and I would love to."

"Hope I am not interrupting anything," Dev said as he came to the backyard.

"No," Nalini said. "Did you talk to your boss?"

"Yes aunty. My team is expecting me to return soon."

"I am telling Meera that Jaya can stay with us while you wait to become permanent residents of the US."

"That's a great idea aunty. Thank you. Meera, what do you think about aunty's offer to help?" Dev turned to his wife to learn her decision.

"I don't know what to do. We don't know when we will get our green cards."

"Aunty, Meera is correct. Indians have to wait a long time to get their green cards."

"Mom, are you sure you can take care of Jaya?" Meera asked.

"Of course," Nalini replied. "Let me spend some time with my granddaughter. This way you will visit us more often."

"Mom, I am very thankful that we can count on you in this difficult hour," Meera said and leaned her head on her mother's shoulder. "We will also hire a nanny so that you won't be burdened."

"There is a nanny agency that my friend highly recommends," Nalini said. "Let's contact them tomorrow morning."

"Am I missing something?" Krishnan, Meera's father said and joined his family.

After the setback with Jaya's visa, worries engulfed Meera and Dev. It was not a small problem to shrug away. Nalini's helping gesture came as a shot of relief.

***

It was exactly four weeks since they adopted Jaya and now they were in the airport preparing to leave for the US. Even though their parents and friends surrounded them, the fact that they would leave without their daughter made things harder for Meera and Dev.

Meera kissed Jaya again and recited a set of instructions to her nanny again.

"Meera madam, don't worry I will take good care of your daughter," nanny Sudha said. She was in her mid-forties and was experienced.

"Sudha, please make sure you are online at 10 am every day," Meera said.

"Yes, madam, I have already set a reminder on my phone. Rain or shine we will be online at 10 am." Sudha took Jaya and held her.

"Mom, if things are not working out, please promise that you will let me know."

"Yes Meera, I will," Nalini nodded. "Now relax and go through the security check."

With a heavy heart, Meera and Dev took leave from their families and headed to the security checkpoint. On the flight, they felt heavy as though they were leaving a part of themselves behind.

***

On the evening of their arrival to the US, Meera and Dev met with their immigration lawyer. Since immigration is a labyrinthine process, to make it bearable, many hired lawyers. Their counsel, Ray Gallo met them at the reception and took them to his office.

After the pleasantries, Dev described their predicament to Ray. "We want to know if we can expedite our green card process?"

"Since you are from India there is a long wait and I am afraid there is absolutely nothing we can do." Ray shook his head. "The good news is this year the visa numbers for Indians have been moving. At this rate, I think you can get your green card in two years."

"Two more years!" Meera exclaimed. "That's a long time. It is not our fault that we are Indians," According to the current rules in the US, there is a cap on the number of green cards that are issued for each country. This number is independent of the country's population. So, people of Indian origin have to wait longer to become permanent residents of the US while citizens of other less populated countries do not.

"I totally understand your frustration." Ray leaned forward. "I wish this country would acknowledge the fact that Indians have been crucial for the tech industry. You come to the US for education or work and make this country your home. Indians are highly educated, work hard and make good money and pay taxes. Most importantly they don't depend on government handouts. If you ask me, I think Indians form the best immigrant community."

"You think that we are important Ray, but some think there are just too many of us," Meera said.

"The fact is that immigrants have built this country and no one can change that fact," Ray observed.

"But some politicians are taking a hard stance against immigration," Dev said. "Sometimes I fear we may never get our green cards."

"I hear you," Ray agreed. "My great-great-grandfather came from Italy for a better life. If it was okay back then, why would immigration be bad now?"

***

As much as they missed physically touching their daughter, the daily video chats gave them some comfort. On the weekdays, Sudha punctually logged into the computer at 10 am and on the weekends Meera's parents came online.

The guilt that their daughter was not with them made Meera forgetful and absent minded. She would reminisce about the few weeks when she was actually with her child. The long-distance parenting had become a nightmare. While her co-workers who delivered babies were eligible for medical leave to recuperate and bond with their child, she and Dev on the other hand had to adjust within weeks. The sad truth of the matter was that she couldn't even bring her child home.

Meera started reading intensively about child development. On many occasions, she went to the child development facilities to learn about the trendy books, videos and activities that other parents were incorporating for their children. After further investigation, she would decide on the best course of action for her child and pass on that information to her parents and the nanny.

***

"Why are you late again?" Meera asked Sudha.

"We have not been feeling well," Nalini said, sticking her head close to the laptop's camera.

"Why? What happened?"

"The usual stuff, cold and fever," Nalini answered.

"Is Jaya sick?"

"No, she is fine. Look she is sleeping." Nalini tilted the laptop monitor so that her daughter could see Jaya.

Meera sighed. Although she had become a mother accidentally, she still wished she could hold her daughter, rub her tiny fingers, shower her with love and do much more. But for now, they were all doing what they could. In her sleep, Jaya threw her blanket sideways exposing a white plaster on her left leg.

"What is that?" Meera screamed.

Nalini froze. She set the computer back on the table and sat in the chair. "There was an accident. Your dad was carrying Jaya when he slipped and they both fell. There is a tiny fracture on her left leg."

"Why didn't you tell us?" Dev asked.

"We didn't want to upset you. We took her to our doctor immediately. Since she is young, he didn't want her to move that leg as much that's why he put a cast on. There is nothing to worry about." Nalini's assurances fell on deaf ears.

The accident and the fact that her mother chose to hide it were upsetting to Meera. As a parent of the child, she had the right to such information.

"How long does she have to be in that cast?" Dev asked.

"Three more weeks," Nalini mumbled.

"Shouldn't Sudha have informed us?" Meera asked Dev after they logged off the video chat. "She is totally insubordinate."

38

"I think she follows your parent's instructions."

"They said they would take proper care but this happened."

"Sometimes accidents happen. When I was a kid, I would constantly get injured. Look at this," Dev said and pointed to a long scar below his right knee. "I was fencing a gate which had sharp endings and one of them cut me deep. Just like me, Jaya is also experiencing injuries at an early age. I am sure she will be fine in no time."

***

Jaya's accident brought out a worrying mother in Meera. She insisted that her parents should video chat twice a day.

On several occasions, Dev found Meera morose and obsessively watching Jaya's videos. In the following weeks, Jaya's small bone healed and she was back to being her usual self.

One day, after he returned from work Dev asked Meera, "Do you want to be with Jaya?"

"What kind of question is that? Of course, I want to be with her." She couldn't tell if he was serious or not. But she knew the question was too sensitive to toy with her.

"Then let's move back." He placed his arms around Meera's shoulder and took her to the sofa in the living room.

"Move where?"

"India," he replied calmly.

She looked into his dark eyes. "What about our green cards?" He started the process some six years ago, before they met. After their marriage, she was added to his application. The process did cost him both money and time. By leaving the country, they would lose it all.

"What about it? The process is excruciatingly slow. I don't see a need to wait so long," he said with detachment. He came to the US a decade ago and his ambition to make it home had been lost in the trail of paperwork, a fortune in lawyer's fee and a perpetual wait that didn't promise an end date.

"Are you sure?" She asked again.

"Yes. We can find jobs in India," Dev assured. "We will not be losing anything, in fact we will be gaining everything."

She hugged him tight and said, "Let's go home to Jaya."

Commission Master

'Gopal, wake-up,' my father shouted. "Are you deaf or what? How many times do I have to say your name before you answer me?"

I can hear everything that he is saying; my bedroom door is wide open, it is not like my blanket is sound-proof. But it is five in the morning and I do not want to wake up. I don't understand why he can't let me sleep? Since he suffers from insomnia, he is jealous about how easily I could fall asleep anywhere anytime.

"Let the poor boy sleep," my mother said.

"He is not your little boy any more, he is an adult. He has to wake up and accompany me to perform a prayer."

"When he was at the priesthood college, they made him wake up at 4 am; can't you give him a break?"

"How about I get a break? I am sixty years old and supporting this good for nothing son."

My father will be sixty next year but for the last three years, he has been saying he is sixty. I do not know whether there is any advantage of being sixty but he surely likes to call himself older than his true age.

"I am tired of arguing with you," my mother said. "Whenever I say give him a break, you talk about your age. How are these two related?"

"I don't have time to discuss all this. I need to get to Venkat Reddy's house by 5:30 am. I don't have the luxury of staying home and arguing with you."

"Come to the kitchen and have some coffee," my mother suggested.

"Yes, yes I need to have coffee before leaving."

I love you mother. My mother is a saint; she always came to my rescue. Such a doting mother.

We lived in a two-bedroom apartment. Luckily, I had my own room. After I moved home some three years ago, every day my father would come to my room and try to wake me up for this prayer or that prayer. For the last six months, I refused to oblige. I don't have to be a helicopter priest like him. I am looking for a full-time employment. One where I would not have to drive around.

***

I arrived at the Ganesh temple at 10 am. My interview with the temple trustee is at 11 am but I came early to pray and check out the temple.

Even though the temple is named after Ganesh, there are other deities. I offered prayers to Lord Vishnu, Goddess Lakshmi, Lord Shiva, Goddess Durga and Lord Ganesh. On the side, in a separate building is the temple of navagrahas, the nine major celestial bodies of Hinduism . By looking at the priests, I couldn't tell who is permanent and who is temporary. So, if I get selected, I don't know where I will be posted, that makes me uncomfortable.

I am surprised to see a small garden next to the navagrahas. My grandmother told me that in old times, temples were surrounded by large gardens but lately there is no space and hence the first thing that is let go are the gardens. Now, temples spring up everywhere. Even under overpasses. I took a seat on the bench facing the garden. I wondered if the priests fetched the flowers from this lovely garden.

"Are you Gopal?" asked an elderly man, breaking my reverie. He had three horizontal lines of vibhuti on his forehead.

"Yes," I nodded and rose.

"I am Shiva Sarma, the temple trustee." He signed me to sit. "I like sitting here too." He took a seat.

"Namaste sir," I greeted.

"Did you bring your resume?"

"Resume?" I asked, involuntarily scratching my head. I never thought I would need a resume for my line of work. I mean I came to get interviewed for being a priest and assumed that I would be asked to recite some slokas and then I would get the job on the spot.

"Yes, son, a resume."

"One second sir," I said calmly. I started searching my messenger bag. After some searching, I said, "I think I left it on my desk. Can I bring it later sir?"

"Okay son. I will be here tomorrow as well. Make sure you bring it at 7 am."

Why 7 am? "Sure sir, I will bring it tomorrow."

"Let's go to my office. I want you to recite some slokas."

That brought a smile on my face. I was trained to recite slokas and I can recite them in my dreams.

"This is a big office," I complimented as we entered.

"Yes, this was constructed last year."

My mind started calculating the temple collections. It became clear that this temple received a lot of donations. I badly want to join this very temple.

"Please sit," Shiva said.

I liked his politeness. I pulled up a chair and sat comfortably.

Shiva asked me to recite slokas from the Vedas. For each recitation, he closed his eyes and smiled. I am sure he is enjoying my magic with words. I had the knack of remembering the toughest of the tough slokas. My grandmother was the one who spotted my talent when I was nine-years old. I remembered my grandmother's smiling face.

"You are very talented," Shiva complimented.

I grinned. I wish my father was in the room. He needs to know how people appreciate me. Maybe then, he would stop berating me on a daily basis.

"When can I join?" I wish I didn't sound so eager.

"Soon. But, first bring me your resume. Make sure to include references. This temple is a community temple and we want to have priests with good character."

"Yes sir. I understand." *Don't I look like a good guy?* "Thank you, sir."

I left the temple thinking about references.

***

On my way back, to satisfy my growling stomach, I stopped at a snack place. "A piece of black forest," I ordered. My father didn't approve of me eating cakes, especially the ones with eggs. But this is my only weakness. I am glad I stopped a little way away from my home. While eating the best cake ever, I noticed an internet café next door.

"Do you know how to prepare a resume?" I asked the young man tending the internet café.

"Of course, sir," the chap replied.

He and I sat at a computer. "I will use this template. Do you like it?" the chap asked.

"Show me more," I said. I am the customer. I cannot just look at one and approve.

"Okay." He opened a couple.

"I like the first one better," I said.

"I knew it," he said. "What's your name?"

"Gopal Varma."

"What's your age?"

"Why do you care?" Stupid questions make me frown.

"Some people are including their age in their resume. That's why I asked."

"Oh, I am twenty-five." What a disgrace that my school did not teach us anything about resumes. If I knew, then I wouldn't have to disclose sensitive information to a stranger.

"I am one year younger than you," the chap said. "I am Pill."

"Your name is really Pill?"

He leaned closer to me and whispered, "It's short for Pillaiyar."

"Doesn't that name get you into trouble?"

"Not really, my friends call me Chill Pill." He grinned. "Have you ever thought of a shorter name? Perhaps a catchy one?"

"My short names would be - Go and Goal. So, no, I haven't."

"Or you can go by Gop." He snorted.

I stared at him.

"Sorry. Do you have work experience?" he asked.

I nodded.

"Where did you work?"

"Don't you believe me?"

"I believe you but we have to mention the places you worked at."

"Really? Let me think." Then I blurted out a few places that I could recall. While attending priesthood school, I helped a priest. After graduating, for a year, I worked as a concierge's priest in a different state. I would perform rituals for one family for a few months and then move to another family. For the last three years, I have been living at home and I have been helping my father with his work. My father sometimes gave me a small portion of what he made, but most of the time he kept all to himself. I didn't want to beg.

"Did you ever work at a temple?"

"I helped a priest."

He shook his head. "We need to list a temple."

"Which temple?"

"Let's say you worked at my neighborhood temple for two years."

"Two years!" The fact that every neighborhood had a temple made the Pill's suggestion acceptable.

After a few minutes, he printed the document.

On the paper, my life looked perfect.

***

Next day, I arrived early at my possible employer's office.

"It is good to know that you are punctual," Shiva said.

"Yes sir."

He sat at his desk and carefully studied my resume.

In my head, my odds of getting the job were going higher. Why wouldn't he like me? I am on time, my sloka repertoire is long and I am an honest guy.

"Did you work at this temple in Anand Nagar?" Shiva asked.

"Yes, sir, for two years."

"Okay, I will discuss this with my colleagues and will let you know," Shiva said rather abruptly.

"Okay sir. I would like to start as soon as I can."

"I will notify you by tomorrow."

The thought that in no time I would be out of my father's place made me excited. A full-time job at a midsize temple, that would look very good on my resume. Then, I will tell my father that his freelance priest job sucks, big time.

I came to the parking lot when Shiva came behind me. "Is everything all right sir?" I asked.

"No son," he shook his head. "I hate to do this. But I can't consider you for the position."

"Why sir?" My voice squeaked.

"Because you listed a bogus temple on your resume." He looked straight into my eyes. "I noticed a slight lisp in your speech but I wanted to overlook that because of your breadth of knowledge. But you disappointed me with your fake resume."

What am I hearing? How can I disappoint this man whom I just met yesterday? My heart began to ache. He noticed my lisp and still wanted to offer me a job and I blew it because of Pill? How can I be so stupid? As Shiva walked away, my chances of getting a job with him vanished.

***

I raced to beat up Pill. But, of course his shop was closed. I sat on the sidewalk brewing with anger and rage. I prepared a list of insults to hurl at him. I wonder by seeding the resumes with fake details if he helps people or jeopardizes their chances.

"Do you need more copies?" Pill asked as he opened the shop.

I smiled. I didn't show my anger. I didn't want him to slip away.

He sat at his counter and turned on his computer.

"Jackass, your stupidity has cost me a job," I started hitting Pill with my resume.

"Please Gopal stop it. I just tried to help," he begged.

"I thought every neighborhood has a temple. What kind of neighborhood is this that doesn't have a temple?"

"We do have a temple."

"Then why would a temple trustee say that I made up your temple?"

"I swear Gopal, we do have a temple."

"Show me," I demanded.

He looked at his watch and said, "I can close the shop for ten minutes. Not more than that."

He pulled the shutters and I followed him through a narrow lane.

We arrived at a two-story structure. A couple of cement sculptures of Gods adorned the main entrance. I entered the temple dumbstruck. How can Shiva say there was no temple when I just entered the one that I listed in my resume?

"Three deities are in the lower level and Sai Baba is in the upper level," Pill said.

The dark interior didn't appeal to me. "I also see navagrahas," I said, trying to be smart.

"Of course."

We went to each deity and prayed.

"I avoid going upstairs," Pill said.

"Why?"

"Because this place is crazy," Pill replied.

"Why are you here Pill?" shouted someone.

I saw a burly man on the stairs.

"My friend wanted to visit the temple," Pill said.

"I don't want you to damage anything around here," the man said loudly.

Pill rolled his eyes. "Last time was an accident. I apologized for that."

"What does your friend do?" The man studied me from head to toe.

"He is a priest, and he is currently looking for a job."

"Young man today is your lucky day, there is an opening at this temple," the man smiled.

I smiled and looked at Pill. He shook his head.

"Come upstairs to my office," the man said and disappeared.

Pill pulled me to one corner and said, "Don't even think about working here."

"Why not? Remember that I need a job."

"This guy is crazy, trust me," Pill warned.

"He can't be crazier than my father."

"Don't come blaming me if anything goes wrong," Pill said.

"What could go wrong?" I shrugged. "He will pay me for performing prayers."

"Now, you are on your own," Pill said and walked out.

I heard his advice like unrelated news. I didn't let it register.

I adjusted my shirt and took the stairs.

When I landed on the upper level, a nice breeze welcomed me.

I bowed to the Sai Baba statue and searched for the man's office. It was opposite the Sai statue. I knocked on the open door.

"Come in," he answered.

I entered the cluttered office amazed at all the stuff. Piles of ticket books covered his table. He was refilling a ghee bottle.

"Do you sell a lot of tickets?" I blurted out.

"I try. Different rates for different prayers."

I could smell his body odor. A sudden urge to jump out of the seat and run towards the door occurred to me. But a hope for the job pinned me down.

"Can you start tomorrow?" he asked.

"Yes, but I don't know your name."

He wiped his greasy hands on his shirt and extended his hand towards me.

"I am Lal Yadav. People call me Yadav."

"I am Gopal Varma." I felt grease on my hand.

"So now that you know my name, can you start tomorrow?" he asked.

"Yes, I can start tomorrow. What is the salary?"

"Five thousand rupees."

My jaw dropped at hearing the lowest possible salary in the city. Even a part-time priest made more money than that. With that salary, I cannot move out of my father's place. What am I getting into? "That's way too low," I managed to say.

"In six months, I will raise it. Don't worry," he assured.

"To what?"

"If you show me that you are dedicated and hardworking, I will double it."

"Six months is a long time. I need a salary bump in two months."

"Let's agree on three months."

Three months did not sound that bad. Even if I continue to live at my father's, my father would see me in a new light, as employed. I would be busy with work and won't see him as much. I might be able to contribute towards household expenses and that might make him happy.

"So, are you on board or what?"

"I am Yadav sir." I smiled.

"Just call me sir."

***

"Mother, today is the best day," I said and hugged my mother. I gave her the sweets that I bought on my way home. Sweets made the news sweeter.

"I was sure you would get selected at the Ganesh temple," she said

"This is a different temple," I said.

"Any temple should be okay."

Mother, an innocent soul did not know much about the real world. She lived in a shell. I did not want to disprove her assumptions. We opened the sweets and were savoring them when my father entered the house.

"Sweets! Did you get the job?" he asked.

"Yes father," I grinned.

"Good. How much is the salary?"

"Come and enjoy the sweets," my mother suggested.

"Okay," He joined us.

I loved that three of us were enjoying something together. I wished time would stand still for a moment. I kept watching my father's mouth. It was refreshing to see him munch sweets instead of me.

My mother brought salty snacks and we ate them too.

"Savitri, can you make some coffee?" he asked my mother.

She nodded.

I wish he let her relax for a time. She is just processing the news of her son's job. After living at home as a second-class citizen, my status would go up.

"So, how much are you going to make?" my father asked.

"I took a job at another temple, a smaller one." Energy in my voice plummeted.

"Another temple? I thought you went for an interview at the Ganesh temple."

"I didn't get selected at the Ganesh temple."

"Why?"

Shiva's face with a disapproving look flashed in my memory. I do have a knack of losing jobs. I did not know how to answer this question without touching on the fake resume. I shrugged.

"It is okay. He got a job at another temple," my mother came to my defense.

"Okay that's fine. What's the salary?"

He asked the same question again and again, just like a broken record. He had a knack for spoiling the best time by asking a mean question.

"Not much," I said.

"How much?" he asked again.

"Five thousand rupees."

"What kind of a temple pays so low? Is it even a temple?" He frowned. "Where is the temple located?"

"In Anand Nagar."

"I did not know there was a temple in that neighborhood. I guess something is better than nothing though."

"After three months, my salary would double." I wanted to make him proud of me. While ten thousand would be an upgrade, it would still be low. The cost of living has gone up so much making it would be impossible to move out.

"Three months will fly in no time," my father said. "With this experience, you can apply somewhere too."

I heard the kindest words.

My mother looked at me and we both smiled.

***

Next day, I came to the temple early. The doors were open. A few patrons were praying. I didn't see Yadav in the lower level; so I went up. I found him in his office brushing his teeth. Did he sleep here? I saw a sleeping bag in the long prayer room close to Sai Baba's statue. I could not believe that he slept in the temple next to the deity. I did not want to know where he would wash his mouth. But from the corner of my eye I saw a metal hand wash sink on the balcony. Yadav walked to the balcony and I took the stairs. The whole scene was so disgusting that I felt unwelcome, I wanted to run.

54

"Are you the new priest?" an elderly man asked as soon as I came to the lower level.

The man's request felt like a cry for help. While people can offer their prayers in any way, many Hindus came to the temple to offer prayers and they would entrust the priest to perform rituals on their behalf. That made the job of the priest so coveted and pure. Being a mediator between the God and the devotee was the best job. "Yes," I replied.

I finished the prayer with a song.

"You have such a good voice," the man complimented and gave me a twenty-rupee bill.

"Did you buy a ticket for that puja?" Yadav asked the man.

"I would have if you were around," the man replied.

"You can buy now," Yadav said and went to the small counter next to the entrance.

The man bought a ticket and gave it to me and left.

"How much did he give you?" Yadav asked.

"Twenty."

"I would get fifty percent of what people give you," Yadav said without looking at me. "Keep my portion and give it to me at the end of the day."

Before I could comprehend and protest, he went upstairs. How could he dip into money that is specifically given to me?

More patrons walked in making it impossible to mull over my problems. When I took the job yesterday, I thought I would be minding only one deity. But Yadav's behavior cleared my lingering doubts and I came to know the hard way that I would be overseeing all the deities in the lower level. I started attending to one patron at a time.

At 11:30 am, I closed the curtains.

"You are prompt," Yadav said. "It is always good to follow the timings. We don't want people to loiter in the temple. I hope you had a good morning in terms of money."

Does he always think about money? Disgusting. I didn't reply.

"Come back by 5 pm," he said.

"Okay." I just caved to a bully.

That evening, before closing, he came up to me and took his share. Just like that I parted with two hundred and fifty rupees. Why am I being so honest? I could have said that I only made four hundred. But, I could never lie standing in a temple. My father would have been very proud if I brought home five hundred rupees on my first day though.

***

My full-time employment made me exempt from my father's rants. At night, my father, my mother, and I would eat dinner together. It reminded me of my school days. I don't remember my father being mad at me then.

After dinner, my father received a call. "Let me check. Can you hold?"

"Gopal, the day after tomorrow, can you perform Saraswati prayer at Ram Reddy's house?"

"Sure father. I can do that. At what time?"

"At 9 am."

I thought for a second and replied, "Yes father, I can make it work."

After the phone call, he said, "Thank you for helping me son. One of my clients had to reschedule his engagement and that resulted in a conflict."

"No problem father, I am happy to help you."

This would be my first solo assignment. Even though I dreaded going to Yadav's temple, it gave me credibility that I never had. Now my father treated me like his colleague. After a few months, I planned to find a better employer.

**

"Sir, I have been working for the last two weeks without a break," I said to Yadav.

"You get afternoon break every day," he said coolly. We were in his office-cum-house. In the last two weeks, I met his whole family. His wife sold fruit in a stall adjacent to the temple. His son supplied milk to the neighborhood. Sometimes his operations were done in the temple. His daughter ran a clothing store. But none of them were as rude as Yadav. It is like nobody can get close to him, period. I still couldn't ask Yadav why he slept in the temple. Probably he will say it's none of my business. I am getting good at having conversations with him in my head. "I need to take off tomorrow," came out of my mouth.

"That's such a short notice," he said.

"I am just asking for a one-day break. Please Yadav." I could not believe that I must beg so much for one day off. This is what happens when someone agrees to a job without a binding contract. It looked like I am an at-will employee, who could get fired for anything that goes right or wrong.

"Why do you need a break? Are you performing prayer somewhere?"

"Yes," I said hoping he will understand. "It's for my father's friend."

"How much will you be making there?"

"I don't know."

"You have to give me 20% commission for the prayers that you perform during temple hours of operation," he said without hesitation.

"Dipping into donations that patrons give me is one thing but asking for a commission for prayers that are performed outside the temple is too much."

"If you go for the prayer, then I have to attend your duties. Yes or no?"

"Yes."

"That means I am covering for you and for that I charge you. What's wrong with that?"

"I will give you 10% nothing more."

"Make it 15%."

I shook my head and walked out of his office. "I am going out for ten minutes," I shouted.

"Okay."

I went straight to Pill's internet café. As soon as Pill saw me, he raised his arms to protect his face.

"I am not here to hurt you." I plopped into a chair next to him.

"Then why are you here?" Pill asked.

"I can't believe that I am working for Yadav. That guy is the meanest son of a bitch." I said it wholeheartedly. I am glad that I am not at the temple.

"I already warned you but you didn't listen to me."

"I just needed a job, really badly. I didn't imagine it would be so difficult."

He snorted. "Yadav is good at driving people crazy. No priest works there for more than a week. I guess you are the brave soul who completed two weeks."

"That guy is obsessed with money. Many patrons donate a lot of things. Sometimes we don't even have to spend a penny on ghee and oil. Last week, I filled the supply room with the donations. The next day, I went to get something and half the supplies were gone. I thought we were robbed. So, I hurried to his office and I saw all the missing supplies in his office. When I asked him why he took them when they belonged to the temple, he said, because he owns the temple. Does he really own the temple?"

Pill nodded his head.

"I thought the temple was non-profit."

"The problem with you is that you make a lot of assumptions," Pill said. "Yadav illegally constructed the temple on someone else's land. When I was little, the temple was small. There was only one small deity. Over the years, the temple made money, so he expanded it. Imagine how much funds he would have pilfered."

"Stealing from a prayer place is the lowest form of stealing," I concluded.

"He doesn't care if it is the lowest form or the highest," Pill said. "He is happily carving a huge piece of the pie for himself."

"When you took me to the temple. He asked you not to do anything. Why did he say that?" I asked.

"A couple of years ago, I accompanied my mother to the temple," Pill started his narration. "She asked me to light a lamp. I lit the lamp and when we went to offer prayers to other Gods, the table on which the lamp was, caught fire."

"I didn't know you could burn down a table," I laughed.

"Yadav wanted us to pay for the table." Pill looked serious.

"Did you?"

"I didn't want to but my mother did. He took two thousand rupees." Pill shook his head.

I exhaled. "Does he have an M.B.A?"

"As far as I know he dropped out of school in fourth grade. Why?"

"Then how does he know so much about commission and percentage?" I asked, still processing the fact that my boss didn't even finish high school. "He is a commission master."

"He is street smart," Pill replied. "He would have observed what goes on in other temples and is practicing it at his own temple."

"Maybe so. Every day he springs up something new on me. I don't know how he remembers all these stupid rules? I am sure he is not writing them down anywhere."

"It is from all the years of experience from driving priests away. He would have repeatedly applied his mindless rules to so many priests that it is now his second nature."

I looked at the clock and screamed as my ten-minute break had turned into a twenty minute. "I have to run."

"Don't run towards the temple, run away from it," Pill shouted.

If I quit now, I am sure Yadav will not pay me a penny. I need to work for at least two more weeks to get paid.

***

"What's your name?" I asked a young girl who came to the temple with her parents.

"Akhila," she replied.

"She is three years old," her father proudly added.

"This is for you Akhila," I said and gave her an apple. She smiled and took the fruit.

As soon as the patrons and the girl left, I saw Yadav approaching me. By now I could tell whether he came to reprimand me or praise me. I had more experience with the former than the latter.

"What are you doing?" he barked.

"I don't know what you mean." Confrontations with Yadav were becoming boring. His insights did not add any value to me and he thought that I didn't add value to the temple. So, we have acknowledged our mutual dislike.

"Why did you give that family so much?"

"Relax. I gave them their coconut back, that's all."

"What about the apple that you gave the girl?"

"She is a kid. What's wrong with that?"

"If they give us a dozen bananas, then after the prayer, we give them back only six. They brought coconut but they didn't bring apples."

"Yadav, don't be petty. You are running a temple not a prison."

"Don't tell me how to do my job."

"Then you stop telling me how to do mine." That felt good. Giving the bully a piece of his cake. That did shut him up. He stared at me for some time and then left.

***

While parking my bike at the temple, I saw my classmate, Rudra Sarma from the priesthood school making a purchase. I did not feel like greeting him. I hurried into the temple.

"Gopal is that you?" asked Rudra.

He must have seen me and followed me inside.

With no other way out, I greeted him.

I went into my office to drop my backpack.

"I did not know you work here," he said condescendingly.

"I do."

"You know I came to visit my parents. They live in this neighborhood." He leaned forward and said, "But they don't come to this temple because of Yadav. Sorry no offense to you."

"None taken."

"How do you get along with the notorious Yadav?" He looked around with disgust in his eyes.

I shrugged. "I am okay."

"I work at a temple in London. A large one."

"Yes, I remember." How could I forget that day of the final year? After he was selected in the campus interview, he came to gloat. He invited all his classmates to a bar even though the school strongly advised him to stay away from all vices. I heard that some of the students took him up on his invitation. Good for them and good for him. Because of my lisp, I never got a flashy offer. A few faculty members reminded me that I should be grateful for getting admission to the school. While my mind wandered, I could hear Rudra saying something about London.

"For how long are you here?" I asked him abruptly.

"What?"

I repeated my question.

"For two more days."

Thank God, he is going to leave soon.

"We should meet for dinner," he said.

"Of course. I can't believe we met after so many years."

"Four years."

"Good memory." I do not know why I complimented him. Am I despising him for being successful? Is that fair?

"Before I leave, I want to ask this Gopal. Are you looking for a job outside the country?"

I nodded, involuntarily.

"Then send me your resume. I will see what I can do. I heard that there is an opening coming up at a temple in London. I can put in a good word for you."

"Thank you."

"Here is my business card." He handed me a sleek card.

"I will." The card looked nice. A pang of jealousy took over me. As soon as Rudra left, I ripped the card and tore it into pieces and threw it into a garbage can. Why did he see me? I wish I never ran into him. I moped for some time.

After a few hours, when I saw the garbage can full, I regretted throwing his card away. He just tried to help me and I refused. My chances of getting into any fancy temple in India were slim, so it is safe to assume that my chances abroad were close to none.

***

After slogging for four weeks in Yadav's temple, I looked forward to collecting my paycheck. But, Yadav went missing.

"Is Yadav not here?" asked patron Krishna Rao. I have seen him meditate in the upper level but we hadn't spoken to each other before.

"I haven't seen him in four days," I replied. How could he disappear before paying me my hard-earned salary?

"That's good," Krishna Rao said. "Tonight, we have planned a special prayer for Sai Baba. We will also serve dinner. You are welcome."

"Don't you need Yadav's permission?" I asked.

"I am sure he will understand." Krishna rushed off.

In the evening, Krishna arrived with fifty devotees. They sang devotional songs. A local neighborhood restaurant catered food for them.

A young man from the group came to invite me for dinner.

"Thank you but I can't come," I said.

"Don't you have to eat dinner anyway?"

I nodded.

"Since you must be here to lock the temple, instead of waiting here, you might as well come join us."

The fact that I am in charge and should lock up slipped my mind.

"I will come after closing the lower level," I said.

I joined the group after a while. They were quite nice. They treated me as someone special. They thanked me for letting them use the space.

"We wish you would take over the temple," Krishna said. "We need someone who is compassionate and accommodating like you. After all this is a temple for the neighborhood. All Yadav does all day long is count money and say no."

More patrons agreed.

I reminded them that I work for a salary and work under Yadav.

"I have noticed your work ethics and I can say that in no time you will be running this place," Krishna Rao said.

I smiled. It sure would be nice to run the temple without Yadav. I made a list of things that needed improvement. The group let me get carried away.

After dinner, some patrons stayed back and were cleaning up when Yadav sprang upon us.

"What happened here?" he asked.

 I gave him the update.

"Why did you allow it?" Yadav raised his voice.

"What is there to allow?" I asked rhetorically. "These are people from our neighborhood and they can use the temple if they want to."

"Do you run this temple?" He asked.

"Don't shout at him?" Krishna Rao came to my rescue. "He was kind to us."

"Krishna Rao, you don't meddle in this," Yadav pointed a finger at him. "You have been planning this for some time now and when you didn't see me for a couple of days, you used the opportunity to host your party."

"It was not a party," Krishna said.

"It was a prayer meeting," I interjected. I should know better.

"You can never host any such things in future," Yadav shouted at Krishna. "Clean the place and get out."

"I don't even know why I keep coming to this temple," Krishna said.

I followed Yadav as he took stairs.

"Why do you have to be so rude?" I asked. "They just wanted a space to host their meeting and have dinner."

"They can use that space for a price," Yadav said. "Krishna knows the price. He took advantage of you. Since you allowed them to use the space without collecting the fee, now you have to bear the cost."

"What?"

He went into my office and took my seat. "The fee with the fine is five-thousand rupees."

"You are crazy. You keep making things up."

"It's my temple and I can do whatever I want."

Standing at the entrance of my small office, blood from my face drained. I worked for a bully for over a month and now he refuses to pay me. I knew there was nothing I could do to change his mind. I felt angry for letting him con me. I stared at Yadav's bearded face and walked out of the temple.

***

"Why are you not going to your temple?" My father asked.

It has been a week since I went to the temple. For the first couple of days, my father did not notice as he had whole day appointments. But after that he started grilling me every morning. He has been asking me the same set of questions over and over.

"I needed some time off to sort things out," I tried a new one today. I hoped he would leave me alone at least this morning.

"Time off from what? You have been home for the last three years doing little work here and there. Why would you need time off?"

"Let him take a break," my mother said.

"Savitri, I know what I am doing," my father shouted at her. "Can you please let me talk some sense into him?"

My mother left us.

Mother, please don't leave me! I silently shouted for help.

"Did you have an argument with your supervisor?" my father asked me to take a seat on my bed.

"No." I did not discuss Yadav before and I did not want to start now. Even if I wanted, I wouldn't know where to start. I doubt whether I would gain my father's sympathy by blaming Yadav. After all I didn't heed Pill's advice and accepted the job. Blaming Yadav would also bury me as my father's questions could lead to my fake resume.

"Then what's the problem? Why didn't you get paid?"

I did not reply.

"There we go. You suddenly stop talking." He got up and went into the kitchen. "Savitri, he is not making sense. He says he did not fight with his supervisor but then why would he not get paid? Maybe his supervisor fought with him. That would explain a lot of things."

That's when my cell phone rang. Thank God, someone is calling me. I reached for the phone on my table and looked at the screen. Yadav is calling me? I declined the call. After a minute, he called me again. I pressed decline again. Why is this jackass calling me? Is he calling me to pay me? I doubted that. But my curiosity grew.

Then he called me again. After a couple of rings, I answered the phone and shut my bedroom door.

"Gopal please come to the temple," he said.

"Why should I come?" I asked.

"Please Gopal. I need your help. Please."

I am surprised to hear *please* from Yadav.

"Before I do anything, you have to pay my salary plus additional three thousand for all the trouble you put me through."

"I will pay you ten thousand. Please come to the temple soon."

"From now on you have to pay me ten thousand rupees per month."

"Yes, yes, whatever you say," he said.

"I will be there." I never imagined that Yadav would call me for help.

I came out of my room. "I am going out," I informed my parents and left.

"Are you going to the temple?" my father asked as I shut the front door.

***

I arrived at the temple in less than twenty minutes. I stood at the entrance wondering why the doors were closed. After a few minutes, the door opened. "Gopal, come in." I heard Yadav's voice.

I went in.

Yadav closed the doors.

"What is going on?" I asked him. "Why is the temple still closed?"

"I can't open it," he said and took the stairs.

I followed him.

He slumped into his office chair. He increased the TV volume that was already on. A news anchor reported, "We are narrowing down on the hit and run suspect who killed a young man. There is a CCTV footage from a nearby store that captured the accident. In the video, you can see a dark colored car hit the bike. The car does not have a back bumper and back license plate. If you know any car that matches this description please call the police immediately."

"Yadav, it looks like your car," I blurted out. "Your car doesn't have a back bumper and back license plate either."

"You noticed it!" He shouted and buried his face into the ticket books.

"Did you run away from the scene of the accident?" I asked.

"I don't know how this happened?" He shook his head vehemently. "Three days ago, late at night I was driving on Raj Bhavan Road and hit a bike. A young man fell off his bike and hit his head on the curb. I thought he

69

would get up. So, I left without stopping." He sobbed. "How am I supposed to know that a lorry would run over him and kill him?"

"Were you drunk?"

He raised his head and started beating his chest. "I am God's best devotee. I constructed this temple. I gave my life to God. What do I get in return? An addiction that would wipe me out. God why are you punishing me? Why?"

So how is his addiction God's problem? I felt like asking.

"Isn't that truck driver at fault too?" He said. "Did you see, the news reporter didn't mention anything about the truck? Everybody wants to pin everything on me."

"Can you explain this to police?" I asked.

"I can't. The boy's father is Malla. That guy kills before he listens."

"Malla, the local goon," I said. Rumor had it that Malla had killed a couple of people in the neighborhood.

"Yes, that Malla. His men are looking for me. They want to kill me."

"How do they know that it is you?"

"I am sure they know. His men came to the temple twice already."

We heard a loud thud. Yadav moved his window curtain and peeked. "His men are here again. Gopal, can you please go down and answer them. If they ask about me, tell them that I went out of the city."

"I don't want to get involved." Malla's profile scared me. I didn't want to be the next on his list.

"Please Gopal, help me," Yadav pleaded.

"I am my parent's only child," I said. "My mother would be devastated if something were to happen to me." I shook my head. "I can't risk my life for you."

"Do it for this temple," he said. "I know you care about this temple and the patrons."

Yadav is right. I do deeply care about the temple. But what could I do? I am someone who can't even get their rightful salary. "What about my salary?"

"Yes, your salary," he pulled his desk draw and took out a couple of bundles. "This is twenty thousand."

We heard another thud.

"Please take everything. Take this temple too." He got up from his chair.

"How can I run this temple if it is in your name?" I asked.

"I will give it to you. Take everything. Please let me escape." He folded his hands. Tears rolled from his eyes. "As soon as they are gone, I will leave. I promise."

I felt sorry for the bully. "When I come back, you better make me in charge. Otherwise I will go to Malla's men." I couldn't believe what came out of my mouth.

"Yes, I will have it ready," Yadav said.

I took the twenty thousand and put it in my backpack. I couldn't be sure if he would heed my threat.

I went down to answer the door.

"What took you so long?" asked the burly man at the door.

"I was praying."

"Are you the priest?" the man asked.

"Yes," I replied.

"We need a priest at Malla's house immediately," the man said. "Here is the address," he threw a paper in my face. I grabbed it before it hit my face. "Follow me right away," he ordered.

"Yes. I will close the temple and come."

"Don't be late."

What a nice way to make a request, I thought.

After closing the door, I hurried back to Yadav's office.

"Did they ask about me?" Yadav asked.

"The man wanted me to come to Malla's house," I said.

"They are doing this to extract information from you." Yadav stuffed cash from the drawer into a bag. "Look at the letter on the desk. I said that you will oversee the temple. The keys are here." He touched the bunch that was next to the ticket pile.

I leaned over the desk to look at the paper. It was a power of attorney, which stated that I will be running the temple and collecting money from the donation boxes. It felt amazing to hold that letter.

After emptying the drawer, he said, "Now I can go."

I took the keys.

We came down and I let him out. I looked back at the temple with pride. I couldn't believe that I would be running the temple from today. Then I remembered the goon's order.

I gingerly rode to Malla's house. There were a lot of men outside his house. I feared the men would smash me up. I didn't even ask where Yadav was going. So, no matter what these men do to me, they would never get a lead about him. I was glad that I dropped my backpack at Pill's place. I told him to take it to my parents if he doesn't hear back from me by the end of the day.

"Oh priest, come inside," someone shouted.

I opened the gate expecting the worst. On the patio, I saw the man who came to the temple earlier. "Why did you ask me to come?" I asked. It was more like a whisper.

He took me by the hand to the side of the house and said, "Malla's son died in an accident."

"Oh, I am sorry," I said.

"We need a priest to perform last rites," the man replied. "We have been looking for Yadav hoping he can help us find a priest."

"So, you came to the temple to look for a priest?" I asked.

"Yes, my friend and I went to the temple several times but no one answered. Before going to another temple, I stopped one last time and saw a bike parked outside. Thankfully you answered the door."

I felt relieved about not getting smashed up.

"I do hope you know how to perform last rites," he said without looking at me.

"Yes, I do."

The Boy with a Helicopter

The flying time from Indianapolis to Los Angeles was long yet Mohit's schedule was so tight that he didn't have any time to take a break or see outside the window as the window shade was drawn down. His mother, Babita had lined up activities for him. When refreshments were served, he asked for orange juice and peanuts.

Mohit munched on the peanuts one at a time and drank orange juice slowly. He wanted to relax and watch the clouds that floated around the plane, but his mother refused to let him sit next to the window saying that 'you will be distracted.' Still he tried to get a glimpse of the sky.

His tardiness irritated his mother. The wrinkles on her face were prominent when she frowned. "Mohit, how long will you take to finish?" His mother asked, turning towards him.

He shrugged.

"We have to practice a lot of questions before we get to our hotel," she said.

He nodded.

For the last three years, he and his mother had travelled to several places. Before his birth, Babita was a career woman. But his birth had changed everything. She gave up her career aspirations for his successes. Every day, she made a point to tell him that she had sacrificed everything for him. As could be expected, it was too much of a burden for a ten-year-old to hear day in and day out.

"Are you vacationing in LA?" asked a middle-aged woman sitting next to Mohit.

"No, we are going for my son's competition," Babita said. "And you?"

"I am visiting a friend," the woman said. "What competition is it?"

"It's a quiz competition."

"How old is your son?"

"He is ten," Babita answered proudly.

"He should be very smart," the woman said.

"He is very gifted," Babita patted Mohit's shoulder. "He was able to read and write when he was just two."

"How could a two-year old write?" The woman asked, adjusting herself in the seat.

"My husband and I were both surprised," Babita said. "He tends to remember whatever I teach him." She grinned.

"Do you enjoy going to competitions?" the woman asked Mohit.

He gave a nod.

"He is so well-behaved," the woman commented.

"Yes, he is," Babita said. "Now we have to get back to preparing."

"Good luck with the competition," the woman said.

***

After they landed, Mohit followed his mother as she navigated through the airport.

"How are we going to the hotel?" Mohit asked.

"By the hotel shuttle," Babita replied. They took the escalators to the ground floor to catch the ground transportation. They waited at the hotel pickups.

"Mom, I like the weather here," Mohit said, removing his winter jacket.

"I like it too," she giggled.

He sat on his carryon and started watching people. He saw a boy come out of the airport.

"Mom, I want to get my helicopter," the boy said, refusing to take a step forward. He was dressed in a soccer uniform.

"Sweetie, you will get it after we go to the hotel," his mother replied.

"Please, I want it now," the boy stomped his foot.

"Okay," the mother said and opened up a luggage. She took out a large box and gave it to the boy.

"Thanks," the boy said and hugged the box tightly.

Mohit looked at the box and his eyes dilated. "Mom, can I get a similar helicopter?" he asked pointing at the toy that stole his heart.

Babita gave a disapproving look at Mohit.

"Please Mom," Mohit begged.

"I will get you one, if you win this competition," she looked at him with a straight face.

That's easy, he thought. His eyes followed the boy and the box until they disappeared.

***

"Enjoy your week-long stay," said the front desk clerk at the hotel.

"Are we going to be here for one week?" Mohit asked rather puzzled. "Isn't the competition only for three days?"

"Yes. We came early so that you could get used to the time difference and adjust to the new place."

They checked into their room on the third floor. Mohit looked out of the window. "Mom, there is that boy from the airport," Mohit shouted with excitement. The boy was playing with his remote-controlled helicopter in the lawn.

"Who?" Babita said and came near the window. "That boy!" she said condescendingly.

"Can I go play with him?"

"We are here for your competition; not here to play with some child," Babita answered sternly.

Mohit loved the way the helicopter flew in the air. Its blue body with black rotor was just perfect. As he looked down, the boy looked up. Freeing his left hand from the remote control, the boy smiled and waved at him. Mohit waved back. While the boy played, his parents sat on a bench reading books. Mohit envied the boy.

"Stop watching and start preparing," Babita shouted. "You have to study for at least two hours, before we go to dinner."

Reluctantly Mohit followed his mother's order.

***

The next day, Mohit saw the boy with the helicopter at breakfast and befriended him. The boy's name was Tommy and he was eleven.

"Are you here on a vacation?" Mohit asked. It had been a long time since his family went on a vacation.

Tommy nodded. "I think my dad went to school here."

"Did he study at UCLA?" Mohit asked seriously.

Tommy nodded. "Today we are going to Disneyland," he said with excitement. "Do you want to come?"

"You can't just invite your friends without their parent's permission," Tommy's mother said when she overheard his invitation.

"Ask your mom," Tommy suggested.

Mohit liked the idea. He ran to his mother who was eating her breakfast at a corner table. "Mom, can we go to Disneyland?"

"We can't," Babita said. "We are here for the competition. Besides, your sister would be upset if we went to Disneyland without her."

"But the competition is not today. Please Mom." Mohit shook his mom's hand.

She selected an application on her tablet and asked, "So who is the prime minister of Papua New Guinea?"

"James Marape" Mohit replied.

Babita checked the answer and grinned. "Oh Mohit, you are so smart."

"Please mom, let's go to Disneyland," Mohit shook her right hand. "I promise I will study hard."

"Let's go to our room," Babita said and rose.

Mohit followed her looking sullen.

Once inside their room, she asked, "What happened to your manners? Why were you behaving poorly?" she lowered herself to look into his eyes.

"What?"

"Why were you shaking my hand?" she asked. "Are you picking up all the bad habits from that boy?"

"No," Mohit was upset over his mother's hurtful words. Mohit hoped that by the end of the week, Tommy would let him play with the helicopter. His dream of playing with the helicopter would be futile if his mother stopped him from meeting Tommy. "Sorry Mom," he said apologetically. "I will not do it again."

"Okay," she said and stood straight. "Now it's time to start your preparation. Today your topics are history and geography."

"Okay," he said and sat at the desk. He turned on the tablet and selected an application. Babita pulled a chair next to him.

***

For the next couple of days, Mohit's schedule was tough and tight. This was his pre-competition routine; not-so-exciting days filled with non-stop preparations and special diets. Since he was still too young, he didn't question the motive.

But his mother was generous on this trip. She allowed him to go to the small park that was next to their hotel. He hadn't seen Tommy around and worried if his friend took off before he got a chance to play with the helicopter. As he was walking past the swimming pool, he heard someone call his name. He scanned the pool.

"Here Mohit," Tommy said and waved from the shallow end of the pool.

Mohit smiled and waved back and walked towards him.

"Did you like Disneyland?" Mohit asked curiously.

"Disneyland was fun," Tommy said. "You should go."

"We will," Mohit said. "The competition would be over on Friday and we will still be in town on Saturday. I am sure my mother will take me to Disneyland."

***

On the first day of the competition, Babita and Mohit arrived two hours early. "It is better to be early," she said. "I know of somebody who arrived late and was disqualified."

An hour before the competition, the participants were allowed into a large room that had snacks and other refreshments. Mohit had a glazed donut. Ten minutes before the competition, he and the other participants were taken to an auditorium. He stood near the chair where his name was written. From the podium he could see his mother in the front row. She waved at him and mouthed good luck." He smiled at her. The competition consisted of three rounds spread over three days. Winners from each round would proceed to the next one and eventually the winner of the third round would get a twenty-five thousand dollars scholarship towards college.

The first round started with fifty participants, one from each US state and by the end of the day only twenty-five made it to the second round and Mohit was one among them.

"You were so good," Babita said and hugged him when he came down the stage.

He smiled.

She hugged him tight. "You are the best. Are you hungry?"

He nodded.

"Let's go and get something to eat."

While he was eating, she called Mohit's father and told him the news. "We made it to the next round," she shrieked.

People at the restaurant turned around to see what had happened. Mohit smiled to dispel their stares.

"Two more days and we will win it," she declared.

His mother's overconfidence worried him. What if he lost? More than him, it would devastate her. For now, he was enjoying the burger and the milkshake.

"Dad, wants to talk to you," she said and handed the phone.

"Hello dad," he said smiling.

He smiled, he laughed, and he nodded as he spoke to his dad. "Thanks dad," he said and hung up.

***

After they came back to the hotel, Mohit went to talk to Tommy who spent every evening in the pool.

"Since you made it into the second round," Tommy said. "How do you feel?"

Mohit shrugged.

"You should be the smartest kid in your school," Tommy observed.

Mohit smiled.

"I can tell you that I am not that smart," Tommy said.

"Why?"

"Because I don't do competitions."

"Why not?" Mohit asked. "I am sure you would win."

Tommy came out of the pool with water dripping, and went to his dad who sat on a pool chair. Mohit followed him. "Dad, can I participate in quiz competitions?" Tommy asked.

"Why?" Tommy's dad asked him to put away his magazine.

"Because I am smart," Tommy answered.

"I know you are smart," his dad said. "Competitions would be a lot of work. You have to prepare for them. You won't have time to swim. You won't have time for soccer. You won't be able to fly your helicopter. Would you be okay with that?"

"No," Tommy said and jumped into the pool.

Mohit stood there staring at the carefree Tommy.

"Here you are," Babita said as she came closer to Mohit. She gave a tight-lipped smile to Tommy's father. "I have been looking all over for you."

"Mom, can I play in the pool for a little while?" Mohit asked without looking at his mother.

"You have to prepare for tomorrow's competition," Babita said. "Let's go."

***

The next day in the morning when Mohit got up, he scanned the room for his mother. He sat up on the bed and saw his mother on the balcony. He got up and brushed his teeth. As he walked closer to the balcony, he could hear his mother talking on the phone.

"Mohit wants to go to Disneyland but I don't want to," Babita said on the phone. "I will take him to a movie instead."

He looked down, disappointed. Last night before going to bed his mother promised him that they would go to Disneyland on Saturday. He went and sat at the desk and stared blankly at the wall.

"Good morning Mohit," Babita said coming into the room. "Did you brush your teeth?"

Mohit nodded.

Let's go to breakfast then," she said.

He ate breakfast hastily. He avoided eye contact with his mother.

"Eat slowly," she cautioned. "I don't want you to choke."

He didn't slow down. "I want to get back and prepare," he said with his mouth full.

"We can take breakfast to the room," she said and got up to get a tray.

***

The questions on the second day were much harder than the first. Half way into the competition, Mohit coughed. Babita looked worried. She sat on the edge of the chair to get a better glimpse of Mohit.

Finally, it was Mohit's turn. The quizmaster asked, "Who is the recently elected prime minister of Papua New Guinea?"

Babita grinned at the question. Only recently Mohit answered the question correctly.

Mohit buzzed.

"What's the answer Mohit?" the quizmaster said.

"It is James Marape," Mohit answered.

Can you repeat the last name again?" asked the quizmaster.

"Marape," Mohit replied confidently. "It is M-A-R-A-P-E-E."

"Sorry," the quizmaster said. "The correct answer is Marape with a single e."

Babita slapped her forehead in agony.

While Mohit exited the stage, Babita met him in the atrium.

"Why did you say Marapee instead of Marape?" She asked angrily.

Mohit looked down. He coughed.

"Are you sick?" She said and placed her right hand on his forehead. "You don't have fever."

He coughed again.

"Is it the milkshake that you had yesterday?"

He shrugged.

"I can't believe you lost!" she said. "You were so good yesterday. You are one of the best candidates there." She sighed. "I was hoping you would be the youngest contestant to win the quiz competition. After all, I prepared you for two years. Two years Mohit! Don't you remember?"

"I am sorry Mom," He said apologetically. He closed his eyes and started crying.

"Don't cry," she said, patting his shoulders. "Don't embarrass me in public."

He stopped crying immediately.

Unlike yesterday they didn't take a cab back to the hotel; they took a bus instead.

She didn't call his father right away. As they were entering the lobby he saw Tommy with the helicopter.

Mohit waved at Tommy.

"I am going to the park," Tommy said. "Do you want to come?"

Mohit looked at his mother for permission.

"Go," she said angrily and went to the bank of elevators.

"So how was today's competition?" Tommy asked.

"I lost," Mohit said frankly with no emotions.

"Were the questions hard?" Tommy asked. "Aren't you the smartest kid ever?"

"No, I am not that smart. However, I knew answers to every question."

"Then why didn't you answer?" Tommy stopped walking and turned to Mohit.

"I am done with competitions," Mohit said plainly.

"For real?"

"For real." Mohit grinned. "I want a life like yours. I want to play basketball, fly helicopters. I just want to be a kid."

"Then catch me," Tommy said and took off.

With his new-found freedom, "I am coming," Mohit said and sprung after Tommy.

Decision Boundary

Jose sat next to the window with the physics examination paper in front of him. The questions seemed familiar but no matter how much he focused, he could not recall anything. He looked out of the window at the playground where some kids were playing soccer. He remembered how he had played in the same field with his friends. He especially missed his friend Juan. If everything went well, Jose would have finished high school last year and would have been with Juan at a college in America. He was deep in his thoughts when the bell rang indicating the end of examination. He turned in an almost blank paper.

He saw a couple of his ex-classmates outside the school building. *What are they doing here?* He felt awkward to see them. He headed to the bike rack. "Jose, wait for me," shouted a girl.

Jose turned to see his sister, Carla. "How was the exam?" she said as she ran towards him.

"Good."

"That's good Jose," Carla said. "I am sure you will pass."

Jose gave a tight-lipped smile.

"Okay I will see you later," Carla said and vanished into the crowd of people.

Up until last year, he was the smartest kid in his school and his family. But now Carla was slowly replacing him as a star student.

He rode to the farm at the end of his town. He sat on the long wooden bench with his backpack next to him. A farm worker waved at him and he waved back.

Watching the sugarcane crop soothed him. A slight breeze blew his hair, he felt like it also displaced his exam worries. He took burritos from his lunch pack and started eating them. He saved a couple for the farm worker who seemed to be working alone all the time. Over the past year, he had formed a silent bond with the fellow. He took out a textbook and started flipping through.

***

"How are you dear?" Jose's mother, Maria asked as he entered the house late in the afternoon.

"Okay," he replied. "The physics exam went well," he reported.

"Thank God for that." She looked at a laminated picture of Jesus Christ on the top of her refrigerator and recited a prayer. "I am sure that you will pass the exams." She hugged him tightly and kissed him on his cheek.

His father, Eduardo entered the house and asked about the exam. Jose replied and went to his room.

"He seems less agitated," Eduardo observed.

"Yes," Maria agreed.

"I really hope he passes high school," Eduardo said.

"Me too," Maria said, turning towards the hallway. "A day doesn't go by without thinking about that awful accident."

"If only he stayed home that evening," Eduardo sighed, "He would have never had any issues with memory or attention." He took a seat at the dining table.

"He would have graduated high school with distinction and would have been at a college by now." In a saucepan, Maria added a few spoons of coffee grounds, cinnamon, water, and sugar and turned on the stove burner.

89

This was not the first time they talked about the fateful accident that completely changed Jose from a bright student to a confused teenager and this will not be the last time either.

***

After the exams, Jose resumed his night security guard duty. The silence of the night calmed his nerves. It was as though he knew all the things that bothered him and all the things that gave him peace. He did not mind the night duty at all. The other two guards who were on the duty were laid back. They all played cards or listened to music. The eight-hour shift always seemed short.

"Good to have you back," said Pablo, the oldest guard.

"It was hard to play cards without you," said David, another guard. They pulled their chairs and sat around a box inside the building.

"I guess once you pass high school, you will not be working here," Pablo observed.

"I don't know whether I will pass," Jose said.

"What?" Pablo asked.

"I was dying to say this to someone." Jose sighed. "I studied hard but couldn't recall anything. I am finished. I cannot pass high school."

"Look at us we didn't go to college but we are doing okay," David said. "You will be okay too."

"Not going to college is never good," Pablo said plainly. "I didn't go to college but I want my children to go to college and I think you should go to college too."

"I want to, but I don't know how," Jose said emotionally. "Even if I pass high school which seems very unlikely, I don't know how I will pass college with my attention deficit disorder."

"There is nothing you can't do if you put your mind to it," Pablo said.

"I don't think everybody needs to go to college," David said as he shuffled the cards. "It is just a waste of time."

"I think you would be better off if you kept your anti-college ideas to yourself." Pablo threw a long stare at David.

"Okay, let's just play," David said and started dealing the cards.

***

During the break, Jose found David alone.

"Do you think I will be okay without a college degree?" Jose asked David.

"Of course," David said as he lit his cigarette.

"I want to do something interesting," Jose said. "I'd like to work for a cell phone company."

"You sure dream big," David said and took a drag.

"Do you think it is too much?" Jose asked squinting.

"No, I did not mean that."

"My best friend, Juan and I always talked about working for this big cell phone company," Jose said with disappointment. "Juan is already ahead of me. He is in a college in the US."

"Do you want to go to America?" David asked.

"Yes," Jose replied quickly. "But it might take a long time before I could go."

"I know a guy who can take you to America," David said and winked.

"You do?"

"I will talk to him and see what he can do," David said. "You would need to spend a little money though. Can you?"

"Yeah," Jose nodded. "I have saved up a bit."

***

After working at a farm, Jose headed back to the dormitory where he was staying. He stopped at a fast food place and grabbed a burrito. He tucked it in his backpack and started walking when he heard someone ask, "Are you new to this town?" from behind.

Jose turned to see. There were four young men staring at him. "Yes," Jose replied.

"I thought so," said the tallest in the group. "Empty your pockets now," he shouted.

Jose looked pale. Coming to America had been more difficult than he had expected. David's guy wanted a thousand US dollars. Jose had to take all the money from his savings and then he had to borrow more from his friends. Then the trip itself was painful. He was herded like cattle. When he came to America, he got sick. He was put up at the worst dormitory in the world. When he got better, he got a low paying job as a farm worker. After paying for the rent and the food, he hardly had any money left. And now these thugs want his pennies.

"Why don't you empty your pockets?" Jose asked, taking a step towards the group. His heart raced and he was on an adrenaline rush.

"How dare you talk to me like that?" said the tallest man. He spat a large wad of tobacco. "Boys get him," he ordered.

The other three raised their arms and were closing in on Jose when a young lady shouted, "Stop it or I will call the cops."

"Lizzy, stay out of it," the tallest ordered, taking a step towards the lady.

"Hank, you listen to me," the young lady said coming closer to him, "if you or any of your cronies put a hand on this poor guy then I will see that you all end up in prison."

The tall man stared at her. He went close to her and whispered, "Don't be mean to me in front of my guys. I am their leader."

"Okay. Then act like one," the lady said. "Let him go."

"Let's go boys," he said to his group. The others muttered under their breath and they all left.

Jose who was nervous and anxious now was relieved with the outcome. "Thank you for your help," he said and bowed his head to the young lady.

"I am glad I was here," the lady said. "Those guys are notorious." She shook her head. "I am Elizabeth Sanders by the way."

"I am Jose Martinez."

"Jose, by all means you should avoid this street," Elizabeth said. "After dark, this becomes a mugging street."

"What are you doing here?" Jose asked.

"I live in this neighborhood, that's why nobody messes with me," Elizabeth replied confidently. "Where do you live?"

"At that dormitory," he said pointing his finger to a building at the end of the street.

***

As Jose could speak English well, at the farm, he was promoted to supervisor. After work, he would go to the coffee shop where Elizabeth worked. Initially, Elizabeth's boss didn't like a non-paying customer lurking in the store but when Jose started clearing tables for free that made him an asset.

"How do you find time to work and study?" he asked her. They had stopped at a fast food burger place for dinner.

"I like to work," she said. "Did you already finish college?"

"I never attended a college," Jose said.

"Are you a high school drop-out then?" She asked.

"Not technically," he said.

"What do you mean?"

"My father wouldn't let me be a high school drop-out," he said. "Do you want to see a picture of my family?"

She nodded.

He pulled his wallet out and took out a small photograph. He smiled as he saw his family next to a Christmas tree, "this is from last year," he said.

Elizabeth leaned over his shoulder and said, "Perfect picture." She rested her head on his shoulder.

His heart skittered. He liked her. He couldn't tell whether it was a friendly lean or more than that. Whatever it was he liked it.

"My family is the best," he said beaming with pride.

"I wish I had a family like this," she said, still staring at the picture.

"Don't you?"

"I live with my mother and her boy-friend and his six children," Elizabeth said unenthusiastically.

"Does he really have six children?" He immediately felt bad for asking it.

"Yes, from his previous marriages."

"Marriages?" It looked as though he was determined to be a snob.

"I think he was married three times at least."

"Do you like his children?"

"Two are okay and others are bullies. One of them, Hank tried to mug you."

"So, you are related to that hairy tall guy?" Jose asked with his eyes popping out of their sockets. They had been friends for almost a month now and she never even hinted that she was somehow related to the thug.

"Since my mother and his father are not married, we are not technically related."

***

"I can't believe he left Mexico without telling us," Eduardo lamented. "Since he loves you more than me, he should have told you."

"He loves us both," Maria said, putting her hand over Eduardo's wrist. They were in the kitchen having dinner.

"Maybe he doesn't love either of us," he said. "What else would explain his running away?"

"Maybe he was worried about his high school test results," she observed.

He sighed. He pulled a postcard from his shirt front pocket. He read the message and turned to the address. This was the first postcard they received from Jose. "Do you think he could still be in Texas?" he asked.

She shrugged.

"Maybe we should reply to him and ask where he is living?" he said.

"I wrote to him," she said with a smile.

"You did?" he leaned forward.

"Yes, I was worried about him and so I wrote a letter as soon as I received the card."

"No doubt he loves you more," he observed. "Did he write back?"

She nodded. "He is in Lubbock Texas."

"Why doesn't he call us?"

"Because he is scared."

"Write to him and ask him to call," he requested. "We have to talk to him and know more about where he works and where he lives."

***

After Maria requested him to call, Jose obliged. During the phone conversation, Eduardo was more than pleasant with his son.

First, Jose apologized for leaving the house without permission. Then to gain the sympathy of his parents, Jose narrated how he was worried about his poor performance at the high school exams and then mentioned David's friend.

"So, it was David," Eduardo said.

"Yes," Jose said.

"How was your trip?" Eduardo asked.

"The trip was okay," Jose replied quickly. The guy who helped him move from Mexico to the USA warned him against disclosing any part of the transportation details. "You will not only jeopardize your safety but you will be risking the safety of others. Promise me that you will never tell this to anyone." Jose promised; he did not want to violate the guy's trust.

"So, are you enjoying your work?" Eduardo asked.

"It is okay Padre," Jose answered. "The farm owner is a nice man. He doesn't overwork us." Though he was miles away, Jose could sense his father's disapproval. "Padre, this is just a beginning. I will try to find a better paying job soon," he said reassuringly.

"I am sure you will," Eduardo said.

Jose was glad that his father was supportive and didn't lash out at him. He spoke to everyone in the family including his sisters, Carla and Lily.

"I don't think our son has a proper visa to stay or work in America," Eduardo observed after the phone conversation.

"Why do you say that?" Maria asked innocently.

"He didn't answer how he went from here to there," Eduardo said.

"Are you sure?" Maria asked.

"I am quite sure," Eduardo said. "I am sorry for ruining this happy moment for you." He went to her and held her in his arms. "If he is there

97

illegally, then his life is at risk. Police could arrest him and lock him up." He shook his head. "We need to get him back safely before he gets into any trouble," he declared.

"But how?" she asked, looking worried. "We don't know anyone there who can help us."

"I will go and bring him back," Eduardo assured.

***

For the next few weeks, Eduardo was busy preparing visa documents.

"How can we afford your trip?" She asked. Jose's medical expenses took a toll on their finances. It was not just the hospital stay that made a deep dent but taking him to specialists to understand his lack of focus in studies exhausted their savings. Even with both of them working full-time, they barely made enough to provide for their family.

"I have to borrow," Eduardo said helplessly. "What can we do?" he shrugged. "Working illegally is no good. He could end up in prison. That would ruin him."

"Please don't say prison," she cried. She slumped in the chair feeling dizzy.

"Sorry, I didn't mean to," he apologized.

"When you meet him, don't be hard on him," she said.

"Okay."

***

As Eduardo got off the plane at the Dallas Fort Worth airport. He was surprised to see the immaculate airport. He came to the ground transport and took a bus to the nearest Greyhound station. Sitting on the bus, with eyes wide open, he was taking everything in that the new country had to offer.

While planning his trip, he thought about visiting downtown Dallas. His friend said, "You are going there to bring your boy back, not for sightseeing. If you are not careful, you could get lost in a big country like America." Eduardo promised Maria that he would come back and bring Jose with him and not get lost.

Before Eduardo booked his tickets, he made sure to ask Jose where he lived. Jose didn't like his parents suspecting him. He deserved some respect for living in a foreign country, so to win their trust, he gave them the dormitory address.

Eduardo hugged his backpack tightly and drifted into sleep. He woke up to a loud noise. He adjusted his backpack and sat upright.

"You mister, this is your stop," said the bus driver.

Eduardo nodded and got up. "Thank you," he said before exiting.

At the bus station, he went to the ticket counter and bought a ticket. Then he went to the wall with the large clock and sat opposite to it. He pulled the ticket that was in his shirt pocket and inspected it carefully. He would hate to miss the bus. The clerk at the ticket counter told him that the next bus to Lubbock would come at 1:15 PM. He had over two hours to kill. He went to get lunch.

***

As he entered the bus, Eduardo chatted with the bus driver and told the driver the reason for his visit. "Please wake me up if I am asleep."

"Of course, I hope you can find your son," the driver said sincerely.

Eduardo took a seat at the end of the bus. He tucked his backpack between his legs. He sighed and relaxed. He took out a small Bible from his backpack and started reading it. As he read, he smiled. "I will find Jose," he said it out loud.

He tried to take a nap, but he could not, so he watched the long stretches of dry land; small towns that sprang up, grew and diminished.

At around 9:30 pm, the bus reached the Greyhound station in Lubbock. Eduardo thanked the driver and excitedly got down. He took the printed map out and looked for the street signs. According to the map search that he did in his hometown, the dormitory was a walkable distance from the bus station. Satisfied that he was at the right place, he started walking towards the dormitory with the map in his hand.

At every intersection, he would check the street signs and the map. He was just two blocks from the dormitory, when a guy came towards Eduardo. Eduardo gave a smile and a nod. The guy who looked like he was stoned got hold of Eduardo's backpack and tried to snatch it. Eduardo dropped the map and with both hands he held the backpack tightly. "Help me," Eduardo shouted.

Eduardo's scream startled the mugger. "Shut up," he said and took out a pocket knife and tried to stab Eduardo. Eduardo used his backpack as a shield. The mugger grew restless, he stabbed Eduardo in the left thigh. Eduardo screamed with pain. A man in a long clergy robe rushed to the scene. Seeing the new arrival, the mugger took off.

"Are you okay?" the clergy man asked as he lowered Eduardo to the ground.

"No," Eduardo said and touched the stab wound.

"I am Pastor Williams, come with me to my church."

"I can't," Eduardo said.

"Do you have clothes in this?" the pastor asked, pointing to the backpack.

Eduardo nodded.

The pastor opened the backpack and took out his shirt. He rolled the shirt and tied it a few notches above the wound as a tourniquet. "Why don't you want to come with me?" the pastor asked.

"I need to first find my son," Eduardo said. "I came all the way from Mexico for him."

"This place is clearly not safe," Pastor Williams said. "I will accompany you." He raised Eduardo's arm and put it over his shoulder. He carried the backpack on another shoulder.

Slowly they made their way to the dormitory. Once inside, the pastor said, "You sit here. I will go inquire about your son."

Eduardo sat down on the first step of the stairs. "This is his photo," he handed over a picture of Jose.

The pastor took the photo. He knocked on a few doors. It looked like nobody knew much. But one boy took him to the third floor and to Jose.

The pastor looked at the boy and the picture. "Your dad is here," he said.

"What?" Jose asked.

"Yes, he came looking for you," the pastor said. "He is downstairs."

"I don't believe you," Jose said. He felt sorry for being rude to a religious person, "I am sorry," he said.

"Come with me and see for yourself."

Jose followed the pastor.

"Padre," Jose said as he came down the last flight of stairs.

"Jose, my son," Eduardo said and kissed Jose's forehead.

His father's wound caught Jose's attention. "What happened?" he asked, kneeling down.

"A mugger stabbed him," the pastor said. "Your father is refusing medical attention."

"Padre, let's go to a doctor," Jose pleaded. He ran his fingers on the blood-soaked shirt.

"I will go to the doctor, if you promise that you will return to Mexico this week." Eduardo sighed touching his leg above the wound.

"Padre please," Jose begged. "There is no time to waste. We have to go to a hospital now. We can talk about my return trip later."

Eduardo shook his head. "You don't have a proper visa to be here," he said. "Your mother and I are always worried about you. You need to leave this country soon. Otherwise you could end up in prison and get deported. Once you are deported, you can never come back."

"But Padre, I just came."

"You can always come back with a proper visa," Eduardo pleaded.

Jose stared at his father's thigh and said, "Okay I will leave this week."

Eduardo pressed his lips.

"Now, let's go to a hospital," the pastor said.

***

For the next two days, Eduardo and Jose stayed at the church dormitory. Jose missed work to stay with his dad.

He was glad that he was sharing the room with his father rather than with some random stranger. His father's snore reminded him of their stay at the hospital after the accident that almost derailed his life. It was right around the first time he was supposed to take his high school exams. His friend Juan, some other honor students, and he stayed back at school after classes and studied almost every day till 9 PM. That night, he was riding his bike when a truck hit him from behind and threw him onto the pavement. Apart from a fractured right arm, he suffered a concussion that affected his attention and memory. He blamed himself for the accident. He was glad that his father's injury was not as severe. He could never forgive himself if something happened to his father on his account.

On the third day morning, Jose was at the back side of a dinky gas station waiting for a guy. He despised the pathetic life he was leading. Though his father's order perturbed him, he was glad that he would be put out of his misery of living in a bad neighborhood. How did I end up here? It was not the life he dreamt when he planned to come to the US. Maybe he should have waited for a visa, which would have given him access to a better life.

A guy in loose-fitting clothes walked up to Jose. He was chewing tobacco. "You want to go back?" asked the guy squinting his eyes.

"Yes," Jose said.

"I don't understand. I never met anyone who wanted to go back. Are you sure man?"

"Yes, my Madre wants to see me."

The guy shook his head. "I can arrange but it will cost you more."

"More?"

"Yes man, so, do you still want to go?"

Elizabeth's face flashed in front of Jose's eyes. He would miss his new-found love. She was just perfect for him. It was like they could understand each other perfectly. "Yes," he said with an aching heart.

"Bring the money and come meet me here on Thursday night at 9."

"Okay."

***

After the meeting, he went straight to Elizabeth's college. The campus was bustling with energy. He passed several buildings and went to her building. A flying Frisbee came close to his head, he ducked, the Frisbee fell a few feet away from him. "Sorry," shouted a group of students. He took the disk and threw it at a student in the group.

"You are playing Frisbee." Elizabeth said as she came close to him. "You seem to be good at it."

"I came to see you."

They went and sat at a bench.

"I don't know how to say it," Jose said, searching for words.

"Say what?" Elizabeth asked. "Are you breaking up with me?"

They had been seeing each other for a little over three months now. Over these months they didn't ever have the slightest disagreement. He was sure she was the one for him. He even met her mother who seemed to like him. In a blink, all this would end for him.

He held her hands and shook his head. He then mentioned his father's visit.

"So, you decided to go back then," she said and closed her eyes.

"I am sorry but I promised my padre."

"I understand," she said.

He looked at her with a throbbing heart. He wanted to take everything in. He wanted to memorize all her features, her sharp nose, her hazel eyes, her brown hair.

"Oh, I will miss you Jose," she said and kissed him on his lips.

They hugged each other.

He was not used to public displays of affection but at that instance he didn't care.

"When are you leaving?"

"Thursday."

They sat there holding hands watching the passing students. He loved the tree decked mall. He squeezed her hand and hoped he would return to this college. He would not only be going to college but he would also be close to Elizabeth. He was tempted to mention his plan but didn't want to disappoint her. Lately, he had been disappointing almost everybody and he didn't want to add her to that list. Better surprise her than disappoint her.

***

That afternoon, Jose was on his way to meet a friend who promised to hire him as a pizza delivery driver. He saw a crowd outside a building. He accosted a man and inquired.

"This call center is hiring," the person replied.

Jose stood in the line. It has been two weeks since he got back. Going to the USA and coming back left him penniless. He was however glad that his father had recovered from the stab wound and would be returning to work soon. Though his parents didn't mention how much they spent on his father's trip, Jose was aware of their finances and he wanted to chip-in.

He wondered what Elizabeth was doing. After he got back, he emailed her and she replied. He loved her very much and didn't expect her to wait for him.

After two hours of waiting, he was taken to a small room where three men sat at a table with their headphones on and another man stood closer to the door.

"Wear this," the man closer to the door said, handing Jose headphones.

Jose wore them and waited for further instructions. The man near the door gave him a newspaper article.

"Read that as clearly as possible," a man from the table said.

Jose followed the instruction. After he was done, he looked at the three. They gave him thumbs up.

"You are selected," the man said, removing the headphone. "You speak English really well. Did you live in America?"

"Yes, for a little while," Jose replied.

"The compensation details are on this," the man said, handing a paper that was on the judge's table. "Call us tomorrow and let us know if you are interested in this position."

Jose nodded. He felt surreal. A wave of pride washed over his face. He walked out of the building filled with purpose.

He went to the nearest privately-owned telephone stall and made a call.

"Elizabeth, it's Jose," he shouted into the speaker with excitement. "I just got a job."

Speaking to her, he felt close to her. He could almost picture her lovely face.

"That's awesome," she said.

He told her how he unexpectedly got the job.

He happily parted with the last bill he had for the call.

***

"I am so happy you got a good job," Eduardo said. "I still want you to complete high school."

"Yes Padre. I am seriously going to prepare for the high school exams," Jose declared. "Tomorrow I am planning to meet my old friends." After the accident and especially after not graduating with them, Jose distanced himself from his high school friends. No matter how many times they reached out to him, he didn't return their calls. Now he felt ready to re-embrace them.

Maria had showered a few kisses on him. Carla helped her mother in preparing a great dinner and Lily had made him a card.

More than the job itself, Jose was glad to have regained his family's love and trust. He couldn't have ever asked for more.

***

Jose and his family were busy with Christmas Eve celebrations. They hosted a family dinner and the house was full of festive activity.

Lately, he had started preparing for high school exams. He was hoping he could get admission at Elizabeth's college next fall.

While he was in the living room hanging out with his cousins, the doorbell rang. His sister Carla answered the door.

"Jose, there is someone here to see you," Carla said and brought a girl into the living room.

"Elizabeth!" Jose shrieked and jumped from the couch. "What are you doing here?"

"Came to see you," Elizabeth replied.

"We spoke yesterday and you didn't mention anything," Jose said.

Even after the long trip, Elizabeth looked stunning to him.

"Actually, I will be spending the spring semester in Mexico as a foreign exchange student," Elizabeth said with excitement.

Jose couldn't believe what he just heard. He asked her to repeat.

"I came to attend college here," she said with no dip in her excitement. "I will be here for a semester."

He hugged her tight.

Just a Commoner

Nanda Kumar and his wife Radha were en route to see their daughter and her family in Chicago. With just one stopover, the itinerary was simple and trouble free. Nanda ate everything that was given to him and requested all the drinks that were available onboard.

"Please don't get drunk," Radha whispered into his ear. "Alcohol is free doesn't mean you have to drink so much."

"I am not." Her request rattled him. He hated her for telling him what to do. But that would be his life for the next four months. He stared at the last bit of whisky that was left in the small bottle that the air hostess gave him. He took a quick gulp directly from the bottle. "Now I am done," he declared to his wife.

For the next five hours of the flight, he slept and snored. Radha slowly slid the ears plugs in. Whenever and wherever Nanda slept, he snored and how could he not catch some sleep on a sixteen-hour flight?

After declaring customs, they walked, took a few escalators and followed signs to the baggage claim. Their daughter Meena was eagerly waiting for them. As soon as she saw them, she waved. They looked tired, she ran to them and gave them big hugs. She took the carryon from her mother and they all went to collect their baggage.

"Amma, why are you wearing a saree?" Meena asked. "For travelling, salwar kameez are much easier than sarees."

"I am used to sarees."

As they were getting out of the airport, Nanda caught a glimpse of CNN footage being played on an airport TV. The reporter mentioned something about the ex-governor of Illinois named Rod something. Nanda could not get the last name of the ex-governor, it sounded rather difficult. Coming from south India, he had known last names that were tongue twisters but this ex-governor's name was much harder.

***

Nanda and Radha were silently seeing the marvels of Chicago. It was their first time visiting the USA and they tried to absorb everything they could. When they returned home, they would be telling their friends in India about their experiences in America.

"Why are you both so quiet?" Meena turned her head slightly to get a glimpse of her parents. Her father sat in the front passenger seat and her mother was in the back.

"We are just seeing the beautiful Chi-cago," Nanda replied.

"Appa, it is not Chi-cago, it is pronounced She-cago."

"So all this time I was saying it wrong and you didn't correct me!" Nanda made an unpleasant face and turned his head to see his wife's reaction. They both laughed.

"I remember telling you," Meena said.

"I like it here. Unlike in India people are not honking like crazy," Nanda observed looking at other vehicles.

"Yes, Appa. Here, most of the people follow traffic rules. In fact people honk to alert other drivers."

"Very nice." Nanda said. He already liked this new country that his daughter settled in.

***

Nanda and Radha struggled to get over the jetlag. After lunch, they would fight a tough battle to stay awake. Since Meena worked from home, she would make surprise visits to check on them. She filled a spray bottle with water and any attempts by them to sleep resulted in water getting sprayed on them.

"Meena, please don't spray so much water," Radha pleaded. She took the free end of her saree and wiped her face. "My saree is getting wet."

"Why don't you and Appa go to the park and walk?" Meena asked. "That way you will be awake and also get some exercise too. It has been two days since you arrived and you have not indulged in any physical activity."

"It is too hot." Nanda said, "I am not used to walking in the middle of the day."

"Walk inside the building." Meena was running out of ideas. She felt jealous of her husband who could go to work outside while she was stuck home policing sleep violators.

Nanda nodded his head. Radha followed him.

"Wait, I will come with you and show you the apartment complex."

The apartment complex was a big closed structure with multiple entrances and exits. Meena gave them a tour of a couple of floors and took them to the lobby which was next to the rental office. The lobby was a large room filled with nice sofas and a flat screen TV.

Nanda's sleepy eyes broadened when he saw a man in the lobby. The man was watching television in the lobby and from his looks, Nanda could tell that he was from India. He nudged his wife and pointed her to the man. Radha smiled and nodded her head. It was as though they found a jackpot.

Meena greeted the man and introduced her parents. "Appa and Amma, this is Bharat uncle. He and his wife are visiting his son and daughter-in-law."

Nanda and Bharat shook hands. Radha was glad to know that there was somebody in her age group if she ever wanted to chat. Nanda settled next to Bharat and the ladies returned home.

***

After a week, Nanda and Radha were over jetlag and Meena emptied and dried the spray bottle. Now her parents were filling the afternoon watching reruns of Matlock, movies of all kinds and news. Nanda also spent a considerable amount of time with Bharat in the apartment lobby.

"Bharat, why are you always in the lobby?" To Nanda it looked like Bharat spent more time in the lobby and less at his son's.

"What can I say?" Bharat sighed. "If I am home, my wife is always expecting me to help her. I am a doctor and I am not used to helping anyone with household chores. I mean, it will be nice if I could help, but since I never did, I can't now. If she doesn't see me then she can't ask me to help her. That's why I am hiding out in the lobby."

"I can totally empathize with you," Nanda agreed. "My wife is expecting me to help her too. I am a chartered accountant and I am not used to doing chores either."

The men comforted each other about how great they were and how mean it was of their wives to expect some help from them when they were not working.

"Where is your practice?" Nanda asked.

"In T. Nagar. I practiced for thirty-five years. I used to see at least twenty-five patients every day. Now my daughter has taken over my practice."

"That's very good. My accountant firm is also in T. Nagar. My clients are primarily politicians." Nanda never missed a chance to talk about his clientele.

"I think it was two years ago when politician Srikanth's nephew came to my clinic. He was suffering from a gamut of problems and no doctor was able to diagnose him properly."

"Were you able to help?" Nanda asked.

"Yes, of course. Now he is doing much better." Bharat said. "I am well known for the right diagnosis."

"Srikanth is my client. My firm takes care of all his party's accounts." Nanda tried to toot his horn too.

For the rest of the afternoon, the two gentlemen talked about their careers. Bharat said how he missed his practice and hated being a retired person. Nanda missed his busy schedule, sitting leisurely was never possible in India. At first the idea of visiting his daughter and son-in-law seemed fun but upon arrival to America, the excitement waned. He wished he could do something to be busy. Of course helping his wife was out of question.

As they were getting ready to get back to their respective apartments, the news about Rod something came on TV.

"Who is this?" Nanda asked, pointing at the TV.

"He is this state's ex-governor."

Nanda increased the volume but could not understand the reporter's accent. He did not know how to turn on the closed captioning. He felt like he was missing out on something important.

***

"Who is Rod the ex-governor?" Nanda asked his daughter at the dinner.

"He was the governor of this state. He is being prosecuted on corruption charges," Meena's husband, Satya answered.

113

Meena looked relieved.

"Was he the governor a long time ago?" Nanda asked.

"No, he was just impeached in January of this year," Satya replied.

"He was impeached in January and he is being prosecuted so soon. That's really great." Nanda was amazed at the fast pace of judicial events in America. "In India it would take a long time to make a case."

"Then a long time to convict," Satya said. "But here the FBI wiretapped his phone from 2005 but the last straw was drawn when he tried to sell President Obama's vacant senate seat to the highest bidder."

Nanda keenly listened to Satya.

"By this summer, Mr. Blagojevich will be convicted." Satya sounded empathic.

"How do you say his name?" Nanda asked.

"Uncle say it like this: Blogo-ya-wich."

Nanda repeated the name after Satya. Thanks to the ex-governor of Illinois they were bonding. The men finished their dinner and moved to the living room to continue their discussion.

"I wish India could put corrupt politicians behind bars," Satya observed. "It is just so hopeless to see so many unfit politicians run for office and get elected."

"I totally agree with you," Nanda nodded. "Some cases have been going on for so long that I don't even care anymore."

***

Nanda would frequently call his colleagues in India. He was glad that he planned the trip after the crazy tax season. Now his colleagues were helping out clients who missed the April deadline for filing taxes. In fact these clients were the high payers. These calls made him stay in touch with his profession and his firm. Apart from the professional discussions, he was happy to share local information about Chicago and get information about Chennai. No matter where he vacationed, what happened in his hometown was absolutely important.

On one such phone conversation his colleague Anant said, "It looks like Srikanth could be in trouble."

"Oh no," Nanda sighed. "Did he trash talk another politician? I don't know why he is so keen on creating a sensation that he lands himself in trouble." After a successful career in movies, Srikanth positioned himself as the best alternative to the existing politicians. With unwavering support from his fans, he won his first state elections. But after serving one term, he lost. From then on, he would come to power in alternate terms. When he was not in power, he would resort to trash talk to be in the news. That was the most effective and least expensive way to be popular.

"He is not in trouble because of trash talk," Anant replied. "After losing the election, he is perpetually in crisis. The ruling political party might attempt to get a verdict in the old corruption case against him."

"I don't think so." After saying it, Nanda was not quite sure but it was better to think positively about their biggest client than otherwise.

After the conversation, Nanda checked all Indian newspaper sites to learn more about the situation. Satisfied with the results, Nanda prayed deeply to his favorite Hindu God, Murugan. He wondered why Anant was a negative thinker. Instead of thinking that Srikanth could be in trouble, why doesn't Anant think about Srikanth receiving a great honor? Nanda was disappointed that no matter how much he shared positive thinking techniques with his colleagues, some of them did not change.

That afternoon Nanda was unusually happy. After lunch he went to see Bharat in the lobby. Bharat was in his usual seat reading a book.

"Bharat I am very happy today." He went ahead and described the discussion he had with his colleague and how there was no proof of his colleague's hunch.

"I am glad your client is not in trouble." Bharat had set his book aside. "You know, a long time ago, I was a huge Srikanth fan."

Nanda's eyes lit up. "So what's your favorite Srikanth movie?" They talked at length about their favorite movies, movie merits and even some famous dialogues.

"As much as I liked Srikanth as an actor, I should admit that I do not like his politics at all." Bharat said.

Bharat's statement broke Nanda's heart. "But why?"

"Because he doesn't know a thing about politics," Bharat said flatly. "He was a good actor but that doesn't mean he can be a good politician and in fact he proved that he was a terrible politician in his first term in office."

"But he has a large fan base." Nanda did not want to argue with a great doctor like Bharat but he felt compelled to defend his client.

"Yes, the fan base is for his acting, not his politics," Bharat observed. "Why are the fans forgetting that the actors make believe and don't write their own dialogues?"

Nanda was visually upset. To calm him down, Bharat said, "If you come to think of it, there is not much difference between actors and politicians. Someone else writes their dialogues or speeches, someone tells them how to act and someone dresses them up."

Nanda cracked a smile. "That is very true." He then invited Bharat for an afternoon tea at his daughter's apartment. Bharat readily accepted. He would rather be anywhere other than at his son's apartment, away from his wife and her help requests.

One day Nanda woke up to the terrible news of Srikanth's long pending corruption case. After four weeks of Anant hinting about a possibility of such a scenario, the Chennai high court declared that it would start hearing the final arguments in the case and give a verdict.

After breakfast, he called his friends in India to check. Meanwhile he also requested his daughter to get his favorite 24-hour Indian news channel. "Appa, I don't want you to get consumed by this Srikanth's trial," Meena said.

"Please Meena, I need to know everything that is happening there," Nanda requested.

She reluctantly agreed to upgrade her cable package.

"I still remember the first time Srikanth was arrested regarding this case like it was yesterday," Bharat said. Nanda and Bharat were in the lobby. "It was my 50th birthday and we were at the Taj restaurant and suddenly the restaurant was closed to stop the mob from entering the premises. We were stuck there until the next morning. As we were surrounded by food and friends, I didn't mind it that much."

"I think it is high time a verdict is given in the case. Srikanth's acquittal will shut down his opponents." Nanda was very optimistic. According to him, the case was long pending and the verdict was overdue.

"What makes you think that he will be acquitted?" Bharat asked.

"Because the case is baseless," Nanda proclaimed. "He made a lot of money from films and he doesn't need corrupt money."

"How can you say that? There is hardcore evidence and the money trail is real." Bharat said. Bharat started explaining popular case facts that were uncovered by the special investigation team.

Nanda would not hear it. He was too loyal to see beyond his client and his political leader. "If the case was so strong then how is it getting dragged out for over fifteen years?"

"Now you are talking," Bharat said. "Because our legal system is slow and people can appeal endlessly and defense lawyers can postpone the hearing dates." Bharat was unstoppable.

Nanda shook his head in disagreement and left. Bharat followed him.

"Nanda are we going for tea?" Bharat asked.

Even though he did not agree with Bharat, Nanda did not want to sound rude and sever their friendship. After all, Bharat was his only friend in Chicago.

***

The next four weeks of the trial were like a roller coaster for Nanda. Favorable news about his client would cheer him up while anything else would upset him. It was mostly the latter. His daughter planned several sightseeing trips to take his mind away from the political unrest that unfolded.

Nanda and Radha liked the Willis tower. The view of the city from the sky-deck was breathtaking. Satya acted as their tour guide and pointed out the major attractions of Chicago. "Look I work there," he said pointing to a high-rise building. His work location made his in-law proud.

"I can stay here all day long," Meena said. "It is so much fun to see the city from here."

Since they were locals, they picked a sunny weekday afternoon for their visit. She was happy to see her parents finally enjoying their visit. Even though they said they liked the other places that she took them to, she was never sure. But from their beaming smiles and their amazement when they stepped on to a glass balcony, she could tell that they really liked the Willis tower.

The trip to the tower was so exciting that for the next few days Nanda only talked about it. Bharat was happy his friend had found a diversion.

***

In a matter of a few days, Nanda was back to worrying about Srikanth's trial. It was not that he worried about his client, he was more worried about what would be the repercussions of the verdict on him and his firm. He couldn't openly admit even to his family that he found loopholes to evade taxes for his clients. However, for this particular client, there was more than just saving some tax rupees. As Srikanth's accountant, he knew about questionable business deals, offshore bank accounts and more. Until now he successfully stayed away from any controversy but that could change. The worries started affecting his vitals. His blood pressure shot up and he started experiencing severe headaches and anxiety. Staying home was only worsening his symptoms.

Meena decided to get help from Bharat. She went to see him in the lobby and explained the situation.

"When did this start?" Bharat asked.

"Two nights ago," Meena replied.

"Why didn't you call me right away?" Bharat went to his son's apartment to get his medical supplies. He still carried a black bag that consisted of a stethoscope, a thermometer, a blood pressure cuff and some painkillers.

Meena was glad to see Bharat with his medical bag.

Nanda was in the bed in the least painful position. He was happy to see his friend. It had been a day and half since he last saw his friend and that felt strange. Bharat greeted Nanda and started checking his vitals while Meena and Radha anxiously looked on.

"You are fine," Bharat said. "I will give you some painkillers and continue your blood pressure medication and you should be back to being normal in no time." Bharat patted Nanda's shoulder. He gave a reassuring nod to the ladies.

Radha sighed a breath of relief. She folded her hands and thanked Bharat for the help.

"Please don't mention it," Bharat said. "I like to be useful and I am glad I brought my medical bag with me."

Radha went to get some water for Nanda's medication and Meena went to prepare tea for the guest.

"Nanda don't let the case affect you," Bharat advised. "I know how much you support Srikanth but this time he might get convicted. Friend, brace yourself for it."

Nanda nodded. As a doctor Bharat was way different than as a friend. His bedside manners and concern showed a different side. "Thank you so much for checking on me."

"Come on friend, get better. I miss our afternoon chats. What am I supposed to do without you?" Bharat's voice cracked a bit.

Radha came back with water and Nanda took his medicine.

"I will let you rest for a while." Bharat said.

"Please have some tea," Radha insisted. "Meena is already preparing it."

***

Thanks to Bharat, Nanda's health had improved. After a couple of days they resumed their afternoon chats.

Now they sat outside on the North West side of the building. It was Bharat who suggested that they should sit out and get some sunlight. Nanda accepted the suggestion, as watching Rod Blagojevich's trial was painful and reminded him of Srikanth's. They would spend afternoons watching people. It was better than being cooped up in the lobby.

In India, after hearing the closing arguments from the prosecutor and defense, the Chennai High Court found Srikanth guilty on all the charges. The court ordered that all the illegal money should be confiscated and the court sentenced him to seven years imprisonment. He was immediately arrested. The verdict created mayhem in the state.

His supporters and party workers took to the streets demanding release of their leader. Some supporters followed the police vehicle that was transferring him and camped outside the prison. A state-wide shutdown was called effective immediately. A new legal counsel was hired to revert the ruling. The party's politicians felt orphaned for the first time and started contacting all politicians except the state ruling party for a glimmer of support.

"I am delighted by the ruling," Bharat said to Nanda. "Srikanth had broken the law and deserved every bit of the punishment."

"How can they arrest a popular politician?" Nanda protested. "I am glad his supporters are fighting tooth and nail to get him released."

"Nanda, your loyalty makes me dumbstruck," Bharat said. "If a well-educated person like you is wishy-washy when justice should be served then what can we expect of others? You should be happy that he is in a low security prison," Bharat observed.

"I am following Srikanth's daily routine," Nanda said. "Today he had idli for breakfast. Still there is no news about what he had for lunch." Srikanth's arrest has become a huge sensation of sorts. The news agencies were thankful that instead of boring summer news they could cover this infamous politician's prison diaries in depth. News about what he wore, his diet, and where he slept was published and discussed extensively in the media.

The next day there was an article about what facilities were provided to Srikanth including a picture of his cell. "I can't believe he is getting VIP treatment in the prison," Satya said watching an Indian news network. "What is the point of arresting him if his prison cell is as comfortable as his house? It seems he has an AC, flat screen TV, a mini fridge and other facilities. It looks like he is under house arrest. This is ridiculous."

"You can't expect a politician to survive without an AC," Nanda opined to his son-in-law's objection about preferential treatment.

"It is not a punishment if prisoners are treated differently because of their social standing," Satya observed. "I thought you liked the American system where all prisoners in a particular facility are treated equally."

"Yes, I do like the American judicial system," Nanda said. "But American prisons are air-conditioned so our argument is baseless." Nanda was glad that he found something to quiet his son-in-law.

When Satya came to find out that Srikanth was getting preferential treatment in prison, he would not shut his mouth. He had made it his mission to vehemently oppose it. He called his friends in America as well as India to talk about this issue.

With the news that his client was being treated well, Nanda's worries had subsided. Now he was busy following the articles about Srikanth's supporters.

"Are you feeling sorry for Blagojevich then?" Satya shouted the question on top of his lungs. Meena came to dissuade the tension. "Stop turning this apartment into a battlefield."

"I agree with Meena," Radha said. "Your political differences have spilled into our day-to-day activities."

Nanda pouted.

"Satya, my father is an old man, he cannot change his convictions," Meena said hoping her husband would understand.

"I am not old," Nanda protested.

"I think you are always supporting your dad," Satya told Meena.

"I am not supporting him," Meena said. "I am saying that it is hard to change people. I tried changing him and I never succeeded."

***

Some of Srikanth's supporters took loyalty to a whole new level. A most fervent fan committed suicide. And everyday news about one or two more suicides by his supporters was being reported. No one knew why any sane person would kill themselves for a leader like Srikanth but then no one really knew why these people really committed suicide either.

"Can you really believe that someone would kill themselves for a politician?" Bharat asked. "As a doctor I knew a lot about pain and suffering. I doubt whether people could cut their wrists or self-immolate themselves to show support for a politician."

"What can I say? Srikanth is a great leader." Nanda was happy that Srikanth's popularity in films had played to Srikanth's advantage.

"Would you kill yourself for him?" Bharat had enough with Nanda.

Nanda was silent.

"I think Srikanth's party wants us to think that many people are committing suicide to protest his arrest but I suspect their reasoning." Bharat said.

"What do you think? Nanda asked.

"I think they are convincing or threatening the dead person's family members," Bharat said. "There is no better explanation than that." Bharat thumped his right fist into his left palm.

Srikanth received hundreds and thousands of letters from all over the world and a few from Indian politicians. Most of the Indian politicians preferred to stay away from him and his party. Any support could result in public backlash and also could affect their ratings.

Visibly the state was divided into two sections, one that felt sorry for Srikanth and the other was glad he was in prison. His party workers were vandalizing public and private property. That was a counter-intuitive way of gaining sympathy. The security in the state was on high alert and police were patrolling streets to stop vandals. One politician told the press that the vandalizing would not stop until their leader was released and consequently he received a lot of criticism for saying it. But unfortunately many political parties practiced fear mongering to get their way.

"I am sick and tired of politicians threatening law and order and disturbing peace," Bharat said to Nanda during one of their afternoon pastimes. "In Chicago, we don't see anyone protesting against Blagojevich's trial," he observed. "The state of Illinois did not come to a grinding halt because an ex-governor is getting prosecuted on corruption charges."

"Bharat, we live in a different world," Nanda said.

"Yes, we are from a world where politicians hold civil peace as hostage for their selfish reasons," Bharat concluded.

"You are like my son-in-law comparing India with America," Nanda said. "How things are done here in the US is completely different from how they are done in India. You can't compare apples to oranges."

"That is true," Bharat nodded. "But should we accept the status quo in India especially when we are witnessing an example to the contrary?"

***

"Oh Maha, it is so nice to hear from you." Nanda was talking to Srikanth's assistant on the phone.

"Nanda, we have a request for you," Maha said.

"What is it?" Nanda was surprised to hear the word request from Maha. Maha was an arrogant snob and he boldly demanded and rarely requested anything.

"We need you here," Maha said. "We hired a new team of lawyers for Srikanth sir and the lawyers want to talk to you about sir's accounts."

"But I am on vacation in America."

"Yes, I know that," Maha sounded irritated.

"Maha, I can talk to the lawyer on the phone and my colleagues can assist him."

"I know it is an inconvenience but sir trusts you and not your colleagues. He is counting on you. What is your decision?"

Hearing that his A-client wanted him. Nanda said, "I will talk to my wife and will call you in the morning."

"Listen Nanda. You help me and I will make sure our party sponsors your next trip to America."

Nanda was happy to hear about the consideration. With the sponsorship he and his wife could travel in first class. That would be a good incentive to motivate Radha to leave early.

"I don't know how Meena will take the news," Radha said when he informed her about the latest development.

She was right, their daughter was upset that her parents were planning their return trip ahead of schedule. "Appa you are the only father who is planning to return early. Many of my friends' parents come to visit their children for six months and they stay for the whole time."

"As soon as the case is over, we will come back to visit you." Nanda glanced at his wife for support.

"From now on, we will visit you every year," Radha promised.

Meena reluctantly agreed to change their return flight date.

"Treating you was the best thing that had happened to me," Bharat told Nanda. "Because of your health, you should travel with a doctor."

"But I am doing well now," Nanda said.

"Let's keep your progress as a secret," Bharat said. "This will give me a chance to go back to India with you and start practicing medicine again." Bharat said and went to talk to his wife.

"My friend is not doing well and he is leaving for India for medical help," Bharat told his wife. "Since it is a long flight, I need to accompany him," Bharat proposed his great idea to his wife.

"You can accompany him and I will stay here." His wife did not care one way or another about his plan. From the moment they came to America, which was a little over four months ago, except for sightseeing, Bharat showed no interest in spending time with her, their son or daughter-in-law.

As much as she was upset with him, she knew he could not sit idle and do nothing. "Let's talk to our son."

His son could not say no. He knew that his father would always do the right thing and accompanying his sick friend on a long flight was the right thing.

***

"Tomorrow by this time we will be in the airport." Bharat took a deep breath.

"Do you want Radha to prepare anything for you for the flight?" Nanda asked.

"I am okay with the flight food," Bharat replied. "If not for you, I would have been completely bored sitting in this lobby."

"Thank God, Meena introduced me to you," Nanda said. "Otherwise I would have gone mad." They both eagerly looked forward to returning home.

Bharat leaned close to Nanda and said, "I decided to go back to practicing medicine. I will talk to my daughter and hopefully I **will start** seeing patients again."

"That's great news," Nanda said. "I think you are a great doctor and patients need a doctor like you."

"I want to propose to my daughter that I can see patients in the morning so that she can spend some time with her children while they are getting ready to go to school."

***

As soon as Nanda got back to India, Maha arranged a meeting with the lawyers. Nanda was tired from the jet lag but meeting the lawyers was a priority.

Nanda met one of Srikanth's new lawyers, Dalmia in a conference room at a hotel. The lawyer was a septuagenarian who solely represented politicians. Needless to say he was very rich and popular.

The room was filled with a lot of people and Nanda did not know who was who. He was eager to get the meeting started so that he could get back to his house and take a nap. Unlike in Chicago no one policed his afternoon sleep.

"Did you give us all Srikanth's documents?" Dalmia asked Nanda. His eyebrows were bushy and grey.

"Yes sir, we already handed over all the documents to Maha." Nanda glanced at Maha who was sitting next to the lawyer.

"That's good. We need to see all the documents and if we have a question we will call you." Dalmia gave a nod to Maha.

"Thanks for your help." Maha shook Nanda's hand. "My driver will drop you home."

Nanda could not understand why he was asked to come to India when all the lawyer wanted were the documents that his colleagues could have handled. Nanda was thankful that the meeting was quick and that a car was arranged to pick him up and drop him off. He was not quite ready to drive yet. Maybe in a week or so he would be ready to drive his car and get back to working.

Meanwhile Bharat had returned to his old practice. His proposal was well received by his daughter. "I was feeling overwhelmed with running the practice," Bharat's daughter said. "I was contemplating on finding a partner. Your proposal came at the right time father." She thanked him. "I will reassign your patients to you."

Just like in Chicago, Nanda and Bharat would meet every afternoon in T. Nagar.

"How was the meeting with the lawyer?" Bharat asked. Today it was his turn to come to Nanda's firm.

"The meeting was a blur. I don't remember much. I guess it went well." "So did you meet Srikanth yet?"

"No. I asked Maha about it and he said he will arrange a meeting very soon."

***

Srikanth's new lawyer, Dalmia appealed to the Supreme Court of India. The court readily accepted the case and gave a stay on the high court's ruling. This news was a shot in the arm for Srikanth and his supporters. Some of his supporters and party politicians organized a celebration outside the prison where Srikanth was being held. It was as though he won the state's general elections.

Nanda was watching the developments in Srikanth's case. He would be meeting Bharat in a short time and was wondering what Bharat's reaction would be. Today they decided to meet for lunch. He was still in his office finishing up some paperwork before he could head out, there was a knock on the door. He was shocked to see a police officer.

"How can I help you?" Nanda asked.

The police officer entered the room along with two other officers.

"Mr. Nanda, we are here to arrest you. Here is the arrest warrant." The officer held a paper towards him.

Nanda blankly took the paper. He was disturbed to see his name on the warrant. "I think there is some kind of misunderstanding." His voice squeaked a little.

"I am sorry but I need to arrest you," the officer said.

In no time he was handcuffed. As much as he was in shock, so were his colleagues. In addition to Nanda, two of his colleagues were arrested too. Even though he held his head low, he could sense the penetrating glares of other tenants in the building.

As they were exiting the building, Bharat stood there at the entrance watching his friend helpless and in handcuffs. "I am his doctor and I want to know why you are arresting him?" Bharat asked the officers.

Nanda sadly looked at his friend.

"We have a warrant for his arrest," the officer replied to Bharat.

"So why do you have a warrant for his arrest?" Bharat asked.

"We can answer all that at the police station," the officer replied. "Bring his lawyer to the police station." The officers hurriedly left.

Bharat went inside the building to chat with Nanda's colleagues who were not arrested.

As expected, Radha did not take the news well. She was inconsolable with grief. Bharat asked her if she wanted to go with him to the police station, she said no. But she made a lunch pack for her husband. "Please help us," Radha requested Bharat. "My husband trusts you more than anyone."

Bharat decided to contact one of his lawyer friends. His friend, Vish readily agreed to meet him at the station.

***

"I am surprised to see the police officers being nice to you," Bharat told Vish.

"I maintain an amicable relationship with the police," Vish replied.

Bharat requested a police constable to deliver the lunch pack that Radha prepared for Nanda.

"Sir, we will give him something. You don't have to worry about him," the officer said.

"He is not well and his wife made this specially for him," Bharat explained. "Please do this favor."

The officer took the lunch pack and disappeared.

"I am very hungry," Bharat told Vish. "Do you want to get some lunch?"

"No, I already ate," Vish replied.

By the time Bharat got back to the station after lunch, he found Vish had already spoken with the public prosecutor to understand the charges.

"Nanda was arrested because Srikanth struck a deal with the prosecutors," Vish said to Bharat. They were sitting outside the station on a wooden bench.

"What does Srikanth's case have to do with Nanda?" Bharat asked.

Vish turned a little bit so that he could see the doctor better. "It seems Srikanth's new lawyer convinced him to rat out other politicians so that he could get a reduced sentence and an early release. For this they had to point the prosecutors to someone who knows about those politicians' accounts. Who better than the accountant who does their taxes?"

"I told Nanda not to trust Srikanth but he blindly trusted and supported him." Bharat got very upset. "So how are we going to get him out?"

"I can represent him," Vish said. "Unless he cooperates with the prosecutors, he will not be a free man."

"So, he has to give information about his politician clients?" Bharat asked.

"Yes," Vish replied. "Dalmia played the card very well."

Nanda did not like what he heard from the lawyer. He constantly looked at Bharat. Tears fell from his eyes. At Vish's request, they were allowed to use a small room next to the interrogation room.

"Don't cry," Bharat said.

"You were right, all this time I was rooting for a criminal," Nanda said. "How can he put me in this situation?"

"I don't think he even thought about it for a second." Bharat said. Vish looked at him and shook his head.

"This is not a time to think all that," Vish said. "Do you want me to represent you?"

Nanda gave a nod.

***

The next day Vish filed a petition for Nanda's bail. However, the prosecutors opposed the bail petition on the grounds that Nanda was a flight risk.

"Your honor my client will surrender his passport. Please consider his health and grant him bail," Vish argued.

"I agree with the prosecution," the Judge said. Nanda was remanded to custody.

Throughout the court proceedings, Nanda held his head low with embarrassment. He did not look up to see the judge or others in the court.

132

Radha mustered her courage and decided to see her husband at the police station.

"I always told you to stay away from the politicians but you thought they were the high paying clients. Now one of them has decided to turn against us." Radha was on the other side of the lockup room in which Nanda was held. She covered her head with the free end of her saree. Bharat was outside in the main lobby.

Nanda looked hopeless.

"Even in America you constantly worried about him and ruined your health. Was it worth it? How are we going to come out of this problem?"

More than the problem itself, Nanda was worried about who knew about his arrest.

"I didn't tell anyone anything," Radha said. "This is obviously not an honorable thing to tell others. I don't know if it came out in the newspapers though."

One day in the lockup and he forgot all about news. Luckily, the news of his arrest was not public knowledge yet.

After the initial harsh words, as the visit came to an end, she became soft and cried.

***

Nanda insisted that he needed to talk to Maha before deciding the next step. Maha accepted his request.

"You asked me to come here to help Srikanth but all along you planned to get me arrested. I always trusted him but he betrayed me," Nanda said looking straight at Maha. He had dropped sir after Srikanth.

"We needed to do this to get our boss out." Maha said with no emotions. "If you decide to provide information then you will be out of this situation soon. Isn't that what you want?"

Maha left Nanda with only one option. All these years he pushed the boundaries and fudged the tax returns and now he could add prison to his list of accomplishments.

***

On the next day Nanda was transferred to a prison cell. He was an established accountant and he expected that his cell would be somewhat comfortable. Except for a hard bed there was nothing. He asked a guard who passed his cell, "Sir, can I get a more comfortable cell?"

The guard narrowed his eyes and asked, "Who are you?"

"I am a chartered accountant. I am hoping you can allocate a comfortable cell."

"V.I.P. cells are for high profile people and you don't fall under that category." The guard looked at his watch and walked away.

Nanda was not going to give up easily. He kept asking different guards but none of them gave him an answer.

Bharat came to see his friend in the prison. As a doctor, he had visited prisons to administer medical exams to the inmates but this was his first non-official visit. He was taken to the visitors' area.

The prison clothes were too small for Nanda. His stomach was sticking out.

After updating Nanda. Bharat asked "So how is your prison cell? Is it air-conditioned?"

"No," Nanda replied.

"Did you tell them you are Srikanth's accountant?" Bharat asked.

"Yes, I told them," Nanda replied. "I guess there are V.I.P. cells with all amenities and then there are others for commoners." Nanda observed.

"Are you going to give the prosecutors what they want so that Srikanth and you will be released?" Bharat asked.

"I have to," Nanda pouted. "I am stuck between a hard rock and a hard bed."

"You were right, Srikanth always wins," Bharat observed.

Hearing that made Nanda resentful. As much as he wanted to surround himself with the wealthy and the mighty, he wanted to be king of his own destiny.

***

The next day, Srikanth was getting ready to get out of prison. According to his lawyer, Nanda should have already started helping the prosecution. Under those circumstances, Srikanth would be released for co-operating with the prosecution.

Srikanth's assistant Maha came to see him.

"Why is there so much delay?" Srikanth asked Maha as soon as he entered the visitor's room.

Maha was standing when Srikanth walked in. "There is a problem sir," Maha muttered.

"What problem?" Srikanth shouted. "How long have you been working for me? Can't you handle a small problem? Do you have to tell me this right before my release? Can't it wait?" Srikanth bombarded Maha with questions.

Maha face cringed. "I have bad news and it will affect your release."

"What are you saying?" Srikanth walked up to Maha.

"Nanda turned on us," Maha blurted. "He made a deal with the prosecutors. He gave them your off-shore account information. He was released last night."

"What?" Srikanth slapped Maha.

"Sorry sir," Maha said, covering his cheeks with his hands.

Srikanth started hitting Maha. Maha fell on the floor, and Srikanth started kicking him. "You are an asshole who couldn't even influence a common man,"

Rescued

It was 8 o'clock in the morning and I was in my driveway with an empty bucket and liquid car soap. I opened the faucet by the front lawn to fill the bucket. When the cold water touched my hands, I shuddered. I regretted planning to clean the car. I turned the water off, went inside to get my gloves, and started rinsing my car. Even though it was a weekday the street was quiet. As I applied the soapy water with a sponge, my mind wandered and without my consent it replayed the failures that I had endured in my short life.

Lately I have been contemplating all the decisions I ever made. I was getting firsthand experience about being an entrepreneur, the hardship and the uncertainty that came along were contrary to the rosy promises portrayed by a few success stories. I was trading one hard career choice with another, the simple act of washing the car seemed ridiculous. *Why am I washing the car in this weather? Why didn't I take it to an automatic car wash? Every day I am doing something stupid.* Thoughts like these crossed my mind.

My stomach growled. After waking up, I did my yoga and I came out without having breakfast. After a thorough regretful replay, I did a mental check and went through my to-do list for the day. I felt that washing the car had put me behind by at least an hour.

As I was about to start rinsing my car, I saw a lady walking on the sidewalk ; since I didn't want to drench a stranger, I released the nozzle to stop the water. I thought she would pass me, but instead she came towards me. From her salwar kameez dress and the red dot on her forehead, I inferred that she was from India. Then I tried to remember if I had ever met her anywhere. No matter how much I tried, I couldn't recall ever meeting her. I didn't want to sound rude so I smiled t and said, "Hello."

She smiled. "Is this Santa Clara?" she asked.

"Yes," I replied. I took a step closer to her. "This whole area is Santa Clara. Are you looking for a particular address?"

"I am looking for Green Barrows apartments," she said.

"Green Barrows," I repeated. "I know there are a lot of apartments around but don't know that exact apartment complex." There were several apartment buildings in my neighborhood but I never remembered their names and none were next to my house. "Do you need to meet someone who lives there?"

"I am visiting my son and went for a morning walk and lost my way," she said without a trace of worry.

My jaw dropped at her last sentence. My eyes searched for worry in her face but found none. I am sure she was worried and wanted to badly go back to her son's place as soon as she could but she didn't show a sign of worry. Her calm composure baffled me. "I can find out where the apartment is located. Please wait." I went inside and used a maps app in my cellphone to locate the apartment. When I saw the red dot in the map, I realized that the apartment that she was looking for is on my exercise path and then the apartment sign flashed in my memory. I put a jacket on and with keys and the cellphone in hand, I came out.

"Aunty, I found your son's apartment. It is less than a mile. I can take you there."

"Thank you," she said.

As we walked, I asked, "Where are you from?"

"I am from Nepal," she answered.

"Nice, a couple of my friends are from Nepal too," I said. Then I remembered friends from my graduate school. "How is everybody in

Nepal after the earthquake?" I asked referring to the 2015 earthquake in her country.

"Now we are fine."

"When did you come to the US?"

"My husband and I arrived last week."

"Are you over jet-lag?"

"Yes," she nodded.

Her commitment to exercise impressed me. I wondered how long ago she left the house for her morning walk. I liked the fact that we were conversing in Hindi.

As we entered Warburton Street where the apartment was, like a tour guide, I pointed her to the Triton Museum on our right and the city hall buildings to the left. "Do you remember that statue?" I asked her, pointing to a long African statue.

"I remember it."

"You can walk around these city hall buildings. That way you will always be close to your son's house."

She nodded.

As soon as we saw the building sign, I could see she was very happy.

"I can go from here," she said.

"No aunty, let me come and drop you off at your son's apartment," I insisted.

"Okay." We passed the tennis courts and then she showed me the garden gate of her son's place. "This is it." She opened the gate and expected me to follow.

"I will come back later aunty," I said. I didn't want her family to know that she lost her way. After the morning she had, I just didn't want her to get in any kind of trouble.

"Please come in and have some tea," she invited me.

"I will come later."

She came to me and hugged me. "Thank you for bringing me home," she said and held my hands. Her hands were soft as my mother's. She stood her on her toes and planted a kiss on my left cheek.

Her gesture filled my heart.

"Aunty, what's your name?" I asked.

"Lakshmi."

"Take care, aunty." I said and after she went inside, I turned around. Lakshmi is my mother's name too.

Even though I only met her some twenty minutes ago, saying goodbye to her made my heart ache. I wondered if I would ever see her again. The fact that she has reunited with her family, brought a smile to my face.

As I was heading home, I couldn't stop admiring her smartness. Lost in a foreign land, she knew her son's apartment number and the complex name and she knew whom to ask for help to get back to his place.

When I came home, I finished washing the car and I knew I made the right decision to wash it on the right day. If not for me, who would have rescued Lakshmi aunty? That thought was unsettling.

Her boldness in asking for help made an impression on me. If she was determined to find her way in a foreign city, can't I find my way in the entrepreneurial world? My confidence that was so low early in the morning, climbed up. I was determined to continue my pursuit. As I drove to work, I wondered who had rescued who?